THE

"I can make more arrows," Lylene said.

"So could either of us!" Weiland snapped—"Had we but time."

"I can make more arrows *before* they get into crossbow range."

"My Lady?"

Ignoring Shile's skeptical look, Lylene laid the five arrows on the ground in front of her. She closed her eyes and concentrated. One of the outlaws, Weiland or Shile, inhaled sharply.

Lylene spread the ten arrows out and concentrated again.

Spread the twenty arrows out and concentrated again.

Spread the forty arrows out and concentrated again.

"Mother of God," Shile whispered.

THE CONJURER PRINCESS

VIVIAN VANDE VELDE

HarperPrism
A Division of HarperCollins*Publishers*

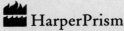

HarperPrism
A Division of HarperCollins*Publishers*
10 East 53rd Street, New York, N.Y. 10022-5299

This book contains an excerpt from *The Changeling Prince* by Vivian Vande Velde. This excerpt has been set for this edition only and may not reflect the final content of the paperback edition.

For information address HarperCollins*Publishers*,
10 East 53rd Street, New York, N.Y. 10022-5299.

ISBN 0-06-105704-5

Cover illustration by David Loew

First printing: September 1997

Printed in the United States of America

❖10 9 8 7 6 5 4 3 2 1

For my writers' group, whose encouragement keeps me going. And especially for Nancy, whose kind words lead me to write this, Mary, who assured me it was worthwhile, and Jane, who wouldn't let it die in my file drawer.

The Conjurer Princess

1

Beryl had always been "the pretty one," and Lylene "the sensible one." There were probably worse things in the world to be called than "sensible," but Lylene was sensible enough to know that even without Beryl as an older sister, nobody would ever call *her* pretty.

It was July, and the wedding ceremony was taking place outside, by the flower gardens behind Delroy Castle's west wing. Beryl wore a lovely pink gown which brought out the goldenness of her hair, the green of her eyes; and Randal had a new soft brown jerkin and matching breeches which were well-cut enough to hide his skinny legs.

Lylene, being sixteen and unsure whether she belonged with the adults who'd taken refuge in the shade of the spreading oak or with the children fidgeting and poking each other in the shadow cast by the castle, stood between the two groups and part of neither. It was a bad compromise, leaving her where the sun beat down on her shoulders. The sun brought out the color of her hair, a color which could most charitably be called copper, though she knew it was really orange. And she had the pale complexion that went along with the hair—a complexion prone to freckle in the sun. She wished Father Tobias would talk faster so they could sit down in the cool pavilions to eat.

Or she wished Aunt Mathilde would beckon her closer, giving her a clear sign that she belonged. Considering that it was Beryl's wedding day, Lylene told herself she was being petty to feel the old familiar pain at not being included as one of Mathilde's children. Not that she was, of course. But, then, neither was Beryl. Still, when their parents had died of the red flux that cold, wet spring when Lylene was about to turn seven and Beryl was eight, their father's lands reverted to Randal, his nephew's son—the closest male relative—and the girls had come under Mathilde's guardianship.

One year older than Beryl, Randal had already proposed to her—on one knee, in the garden, with one of the servants at a discreet distance strumming a lute, all according to Beryl's directions—by the time he was eleven.

And now here they all were.

In the stillness of the moment after Father

Tobias finally pronounced Randal and Beryl husband and wife, Lylene thought she heard the whinny of a horse behind her, beyond the garden wall. She glanced in that direction, though she knew all of Randal's knights were here; and besides, there was only forest beyond the wall—the only road ran north and south beyond the front gate.

But as she turned, an arrow sped out of the forest, close enough that she could hear the hiss of its passing—it happened too fast to see—and she heard the thud as it hit.

What the arrow hit was Randal.

Randal, who at the best of times wore an expression of vacant bewilderment, looked more surprised than anything else. He let go of Beryl's hand and slowly, slowly sank between tables set out with cold meats and steaming pies and other feastday treats.

A bowl clattered to the ground after him. Dish and cover hit separately: two distinct sounds in a silence so complete Lylene could tell which was which in the moment before at least two dozen armed men began leaping their horses over the wall.

Beryl screamed.

Someone knocked Lylene aside—one of the knights, Randal's friends—as he ran toward the castle, where their chainmail and weapons were.

But there wouldn't be time before the attackers were on them. Even Lylene could see that.

Wedding guests and servants began to run, knocking over tables, trampling those who moved more slowly. Voices raised in terror and dismay and momentarily blocked the sound of horses' hooves tearing up the garden.

Lylene fought against her own inclination to flee. A clearing formed around Beryl and her fallen husband: There was no telling yet whether the Lord of Delroy Castle had been the first victim by chance or intent. Yet Beryl stood exactly where she'd been standing all along, still screaming: a perfect target in the quickly emptying garden.

With a cry of exasperation, Lylene pushed against the press of the crowd, trying to get to Beryl. The adults were no help at all. Not that it was fair to blame them. Nobody in this secluded corner of Dorstede was used to violence and murder. Delroy Castle stood quiet and in a greater state of disrepair than could have been permitted in almost any other region and few of the knights had ever fought outside a jousting field.

So who were these armed men, and what could they possibly want?

The tone and pitch of the screams heightened as the first of the horsemen began riding down the slowest stragglers.

"Beryl!" Lylene was tall, too tall, Aunt

Mathilde had always complained, but at least she could see over the heads of many in the crowd. Still, Beryl was temporarily lost in the swirl of confusion.

Then suddenly the flow of wedding guests had surged past her and she was in the area of calm. She didn't look behind, knowing what she'd see—the horsemen, almost on her heels. "Beryl!" she called, hoping to snap her sister out of her shock and into flight.

But Beryl, seventeen and pretty and used to being fussed over, only stood there in her persimmon pink gown dappled with Randal's blood, perhaps waiting for someone to come and make things right again. Screaming. Drawing attention to herself. Letting the raiders know where she was and—should that be their interest—who she had to be.

"Beryl!" It took all Lylene's resolve, and she barely got the name out when a booted foot struck her high on the back, between her shoulder blades, and sent her sprawling. Blackness edged her vision, threatening to engulf her.

Hooves did not pound the life out of her, and her vision came back as she raised her face.

The man was not interested in her. He had his horse aimed directly at Beryl, Beryl who had finally—finally—stopped screaming and now stared at him with eyes gone wide, waiting for whatever would come.

Stupid, helpless . . . Lylene, flat on her stomach, couldn't get enough air to breathe, much less shout a warning. Where were the Dorstede knights?

The man caught Beryl around the waist, pulled her up in front of him, and she never even struggled.

It was Aunt Mathilde who reacted.

"Beast!" screamed their guardian, Randal's mother, suddenly at the horseman's side. "Murderer!" She beat at the raider's leg with her bare hands. "Murderer!"

He bumped his horse against her so that she staggered backward. But as he raised his arm to gather his men, she came at him again, tears streaming down her wrinkled face, all the while screaming, "Murderer! Murderer!"

Keep back, Lylene wished at her, struggling to get to her feet, but her legs shook and wouldn't support her.

The man kicked Mathilde in the chest. Then he started to ease his horse backward, out of the clutter of fallen tables and broken dishes, back in the direction of the garden wall, toward the forest from which they had ridden.

And still Aunt Mathilde came after him.

"No!" Lylene used up what breath she had been able to catch, then watched helplessly as her aunt, clutching at the top of her gown with one hand, used her other fist to pound against the horse's rump.

The animal, caparisoned in thick brocades, hardly flinched. But the man's face, that visible between his helmet and his thin blond moustache, paled with rage. Lylene saw his blue eyes narrow, and he raised his sword.

Beryl finally found her voice again. "No," she murmured, and—almost as though for her sake—the man let Aunt Mathilde go with another kick in the chest.

As the old woman fell, he put his heels to his horse's sides, and headed back the way they had come. The other men followed, leaping their mounts over the scattered bodies and the debris of the wedding feast.

Leaving. Whatever they had come here for, it was accomplished. Randal dead. Beryl taken. Gingerly, Lylene sat up. She had to close her eyes to keep the horizon from dipping and rising. Only by crawling could she make it to Mathilde's side. Fighting a wave of dizzy nausea, she put her arms around her.

Several of the riders were taking women with them: castle servants and wedding guests indiscriminantly. A few of those taken struggled; most, like Beryl, did not. Perhaps they were dazed; perhaps they hoped that if they didn't resist they would be allowed, eventually, to return.

The raiding party stopped at the wall, facing around. Lylene became aware of galloping horses from behind, the direction of the castle's stables: the Dorstede knights.

Finally, the Dorstede knights.

With cool deliberation, the leader of the raiders moved the point of his dagger to Beryl's throat.

Randal's men pulled to a stop.

One by one the raiders had their horses leap over the wall, and then they disappeared into the surrounding forest.

Lylene clenched her fists, recognizing the helplessness of the situation but still hoping *some*body would do *some*thing.

The leader was the last. Smiling sardonically, he sheathed his knife, then wheeled about and urged his mount over the wall, and all that remained was the July sun glinting off the armor of the helpless Dorstede knights.

2

It was probably after the start of the new year, though most likely not yet Twelfth Day. Lylene had begun to lose track.

About six months had passed since her sister's wedding day. "Wait," everyone had told her. "We know who the abductor is," they told her: "Theron of Saldemar is the one who has her. He'll ask for a ransom, and Beryl will be returned safely."

Six months.

And in that time, Aunt Mathilde had died of her injuries and the Church had recognized Theron as Beryl's husband and therefore entitled to all the lands she had inherited as Randal's widow.

Lylene had had enough of waiting.

Now, with the snow swirling around her, she stood in front of the house, the last house on the last street before the town disappeared into the hillside that gave the place its name,

Cragsfall. It was large for a town house, and stone—remarkable in itself. She had seen the house during the day, before she had gathered enough courage to approach, and she'd seen that it was entirely constructed of white marble, finer than any castle or cathedral she had ever heard of. A gust of snow momentarily obliterated the ornately carved door, and she pulled her cloak more tightly around her, aware that with it slapping in the wind she looked like a scarecrow. The bell in the church tower rang the last warning before curfew, the closing of the town gate.

Lylene raised her hand to knock, and silently the door swung inward. She waited for a servant to invite her in, but there was no servant, no invitation. There was, in fact, no hand on the door.

What else should she have expected at a wizard's house?

She stepped inside. The hall flared into brightness as hundreds of candles burst into flame spontaneously. The light glinted off polished gold and brass, off mirrors and almost translucent marble. Lylene squinted against the brightness, temporarily bedazzled and off balance.

A young man stood in the hallway, not near enough to the door that he could have been the one to open it, but near enough that she could see him clearly. Which was no doubt exactly his intention. He gave a condescending smile, as though waiting for her to notice how tall and handsome he was, and only then he made a dismissive gesture with his hand, and the door swung shut behind her.

She tried not to jump, but he probably saw that she did. He'd probably arranged everything just so she would.

He approached, his robe of gold and white brocade trailing behind on a floor as smooth and highly polished as the walls. On first seeing him, she had been surprised: blue-eyed, with dark hair and a trim beard, no older than thirty—as though wizards were born wizened and old. But up close he was much more what she had expected. Cruel, she judged by his eyes; vain, spoiled.

"Lady Lylene Delroy of Dorstede," he greeted her.

Oily, she added to her list, before thinking there was no way he should know her name. "Yes."

The smile widened. "Come seeking my help in a matter of rescue and revenge."

"Yes." He was moving too close, and she retreated until she found her back pressed against the closed door.

He placed his hand on the door, almost brushing her shoulder, almost brushing her cheek, and braced his arm in a gesture that could have been casual except that it caged her in. She flinched. She'd had nightmares, since Beryl had been taken, of what Beryl must be going through. "And offering . . . what, exactly, in exchange?"

Her voice betrayed her, coming out an embarrassing mouse's squeak: "The lands and properties of Delroy."

"What, all of them?" She recognized the sarcasm in that tone of amazement. "Very generous terms. Considering they're not yours to offer."

The words came before she had a chance to think: "They will be if you're half as good as you seem to think you are."

There was a jagged flash of lightning, a crash of thunder. The singed air crackled. She had to brace herself, to keep from being swept off her feet as a blast of wind extinguished the candles and hurled racks of them against walls and floor. Lylene's hair whipped about, stinging her eyes. The wizard, his face all bone-white and shadows in the lightning-light, stood with folded arms in the center of the storm, looking much like the picture in Father Tobias's illuminated Bible of a calm Jesus amidst the tempest at sea.

The indoors gale calmed. The thunder lowered to a sulky rumble, then faded away. The candles, those that had survived, re-lit themselves and flickered more brightly to compensate for their decreased numbers.

"Oh, I'm good," the wizard said. "The question is, can you afford me?"

She didn't tell him that she had no money, that she had left Delroy with nothing except the clothes she wore, which was Father Tobias's charity, for she was entitled to nothing. She told him: "I'm not even convinced that I *will* hire you. How do I know you can help me? You don't even know what I want done."

The wizard laughed, sending a chill skittering around the back of her neck and shoulders. "Oh, you will hire me. You have nowhere else to go. The Bishop of Glastonbury refuses to see you. The Archbishop won't let you past his most minor functionaries. The local lords and barons have laughed you out of their halls. You've sent a letter to the Pope, but timeliness is not one of his virtues, and you can probably expect to wait a year or two before you get an answer from him. I'm assuming he won't have much to say, but if you want to wait, that's your business. I'll still be here, though my fee will no doubt have risen." He had taken hold of her arm and was guiding her toward the door.

"Let go of me." Lylene hated being touched by him. She yanked free and glared.

"True or not?" he asked, smirking.

She didn't want to talk about the Church and how they couldn't help. Father Tobias was the only decent one of the lot. Theron of Saldemar obviously had bought friends in high places—and she estimated that this included the Bishop of Glastonbury. Why else would he insist that Beryl had agreed to the wedding of her own free will, and yet not force Theron to allow Lylene to see her? Why else had Theron's penance for killing Randal been no greater than to donate one year's revenues from the property Theron had gained by that killing?

She pressed against the door to put more distance between herself and the wizard. "How do you know so much about me?" she demanded.

He held his hand out, palm up, which meant he didn't know everything.

"I don't want a mere spell or potion," she said. "I want to learn magic. How long will that take?"

"Ooo," he said in mock awe. "The lady would be a conjurer. How much money do you have?"

"Well . . ."

His eyes narrowed suspiciously. "You've wasted my time," he growled, his voice getting louder with each word, "and you have no money?"

"I was hoping I could work for you," she started, "I can—"

He spun her around and flung open the door, manually this time, no spell. "I prefer my women to be women," he said. "You're too young."

Lylene was aghast at what he thought she'd been offering. She planted her feet in the doorway. "I wasn't—"

"Except when I want children. And for that you're too old." He shoved, which loosened her hold on the door frame.

"That's disgust—"

"And in any case, you're not pretty enough." He slammed the door shut.

Who needed him anyway?

Except that she couldn't go anywhere because the door had caught the trailing edge of her cloak. Tugging didn't help. It was too firmly held to work loose without ripping. "You revolting, horrid creature!" She kicked the door, which hurt her more than the door. She stood there, while the snow swirled around her. Already she'd begun to shiver.

"Hey!" called a voice from the street.

Lylene whirled. Two men. One carrying a lantern: town watch. For one instant, she was relieved, thinking that they might help her.

Then the one without the light pointed his finger at her. "Wench! Here!" He indicated directly in front of him.

Lylene felt the door at her back. She could guess what they thought, seeing her beating at the wizard's door, screaming at him.

"Get over here," the man on the street bellowed.

Lylene turned her back to them, leaning her head on the wooden door. She heard the crunch of snow—the guardsmen approaching. From beneath her arm, she could see the lantern swinging wildly as the men waded through the snow, momentarily illuminating sections of the night, briefly outlining the snowflakes caught in its glare. "I'll work for you"—she didn't raise her voice, for if the wizard wasn't listening, all was lost anyway—"I'll cook, I'll clean, I'll chop wood, I'll run errands." She had done all of those since leaving Dorstede, to earn her keep. "I'll work as hard as any two people, for as long as you say. If you'll just teach me magic."

The snow fell on her hair, on her eyelashes. She could hear the annoyed huffing of the approaching men.

The wizard's voice came from the other side of the door. "What's the magic word?"

She raised her head, amazed to hear him when, truth to tell, she had already given up. "What?"

The light from the lantern fell upon her, upon her hand pressed expectantly against the door.

"Now look here, you . . ." one of the men said, slightly out of breath.

"The magic word . . ." the wizard insisted.

"Please," Lylene whispered. "Please let me in."

The door swung open, unaided. She spared no glance for the reaction of the townsmen. The handsome wizard stood there smiling, his arms held wide. "Why certainly," he said. "Of course. Come in, my dear."

3

The wizard's name was Harkta. Or at least the name he told her to call him was Harkta. Lylene gathered there were names and there were *Names.*

"You can be my scullery princess," he said.

"I'm not a princess," she told him, but he was too impressed by his own wit to stop.

"A scullery princess in training to become a conjurer princess."

She said: "I want our agreement in writing."

He gave a skeptical look. "Women in Dorstede are taught how to read?"

Of course they weren't. Most men couldn't read. "I want it in writing anyway," she insisted.

Harkta flung his hand open, and a scroll of parchment appeared before her eyes. He held it open against the wall, his finger poised as though it were the writing implement. "What do you wish me to say?"

"I, known as Harkta . . ." she started.

He rolled his eyes, but red symbols and squiggles that certainly looked like letters flowed from the tip of his finger onto the parchment.

She watched over his shoulder. ". . . will teach Lylene Delroy . . . everything there is to know about magic—"

Harkta snorted. "*Everything*. I can't do that."

"You don't know everything about magic?"

He refused to take offense. "Nobody does."

"All right, then, write: . . . everything I know about magic . . ."

Harkta shook his head again. "You're out of your depth, girl. You're getting into things about which you know nothing. Do you think magic is a list of rules and formulae I can teach you to rattle off, like the books of the Bible—Genesis, Exodus . . . when you get to the Apocalypse you're done . . . congratulations, now you're a wizard? It's a matter of skill, girl, of balances, of inner resolve and strength."

"Then it's not teachable?"

Harkta made a blasphemous comment that turned Lylene's cheeks red, even here, this far from home, in this room, for these purposes. Then he said: "Of course it's *teachable*. I said I'd teach you, didn't I? I'm just saying conjuring is not as simple as you seem to think."

A sudden suspicion dawned. "Just how long will this *teaching* take?"

Harkta stroked his moustache and gazed through her. "One day, two at the most."

She glared at him, still suspicious. "Write this: I will teach Lylene Delroy everything she can learn from me about magic, and I will teach her as quickly as I can, beginning as soon as I can."

Harkta evaluated this, bowed his head with exaggerated formality, and began writing. "There," he said, signing with a flourish: "The Wizard Harkta of Cragsfall." He blew on the paper to dry the ink, if that's what it was, then resumed writing. "And," he recited slowly as he wrote, "in return for these 'magic lessons,' and until such time as they are completed, I, Lylene Delroy, agree to work for the wizard known as Harkta at such household tasks as he shall stipulate, including but not limited to helping him with wizardly pursuits." He looked at her, looked at the parchment, then added, ". . . with a cooperative attitude and cheerful demeanor. Signed: Lylene Delroy, formerly of Dorstede." He grinned, showing a vast quantity of white, even teeth, then said, "Make your mark here."

Lylene touched her hand to the contract, leaving behind a smear that looked like blood. "Read your part out loud. I want you to say it so it counts even if you didn't really write it."

He gave a look that said he was shocked and hurt by her suspicions, and read her words back to her. "Now repeat your part," he said smugly.

A day, she told herself, two at the most.

He handed her the document before she realized that since he had magically made it appear, he could just as well magically make it disappear. With no place safe to put it, she crumpled the parchment, then threw it into the fire. "There, now it's in both our hearts." She hoped it didn't sound as foolish to him as it sounded to her.

The wizard laughed at her. "As you please."

And she certainly didn't like the way he kept on laughing, even as he walked away from her down the hall.

Her room was cramped and dusty. And cold enough that she could see her breath. There was firewood for tonight behind the kitchen, Harkta told her, but from now on she would have to gather it on her own: for her room, his, the hall, his consultation room, for the cook's room, and for the kitchen. She was surprised and pleased to hear there was a cook.

She scrubbed down the walls and floors of her room, which were simple stone, not marble. She changed the straw in the mattress, laundered the blankets, cleaned out the hearth, all requiring about three hundred trips up and down the stairs to fetch fresh water.

The rest of the house wasn't very clean either, she noted on her way through. The cook was quite elderly and apparently didn't see well enough to clean thoroughly. Lylene guessed the woman must have worked for his family for years and so Harkta kept her on despite her failing eyesight, for which she liked him a little better than she would otherwise.

She liked him a little less when he told her that before she went to bed she must clean up the spilled candles in the front hall. She bit her tongue and didn't point out that it was his own bad temper which had caused that particular mess.

At first she thought she'd gotten lost in the house. Hadn't the front hall been much larger than this? And surely there had been glass mirrors on the walls: She'd noticed them particularly and been impressed, glass being so rare. But now, up close, she saw they were only hammered metal. No, it had to be the wrong room—the walls were stone, just as in her room, despite the dozen or so candles strewn about in congealed puddles of dried wax, looking like a lesser version of what she had seen happen when the wizard had caused an indoor gale which had knocked over hundreds of candles.

Shaking her head to clear it, she stepped back out of the room.

And noticed that the stairs she'd been going up and down all evening were no longer marble either. They hadn't been, now that she thought about it, since about the time Harkta had gone up to bed.

So. He could work magical illusions. It was a good thing she had had him declare their contract out loud. She reentered the hall and began to scrape up the wax. With so few candles, her work would be easier.

Two days, she told herself, at the worst.

4

She got up the next morning at dawn, so that Harkta couldn't claim their contract was invalid because she was lazy. She built up the fire in the kitchen hearth, then gave all the pots and dishes a good scrubbing.

"Too much energy," the cook complained, shaking her head.

Once breakfast was ready, Lylene put Harkta's on a tray and brought it up to his room. "It's morning," she greeted him, forcing herself to smile.

"Marvelous," he grunted. "Let me eat in peace." He gestured her out.

After what seemed a reasonable time she returned to his room but found him instead in what he alternately called his "workroom" or his "consultation room." She glanced around at all the books and maps and glass containers. Soon she would know all about them.

She cleared her throat, and Harkta, sitting by

the window leafing through one of the books, glanced up.

Then resumed reading.

"It's morning."

Turning a page, he murmured, "So it is."

"Harkta, you promised."

"Promised what?"

"To teach me magic."

"Yes."

"You said you'd teach me as soon as you could."

"Yes."

"It's morning!" Lylene's voice cracked.

"Yes," he said, still never glancing her way. "Wrong morning."

"What?"

With a sigh, Harkta marked his place and closed the book. "I will explain once, then it's up to you to fulfill your part of the bargain. I said, and I quote, 'I, known as Harkta'—that's me—'will teach Lylene Delroy'—that's you—'everything she can learn from me about magic, and I will teach her as quickly as I can, beginning as soon as I can.' Correct?"

Lylene just glared.

"Your . . . shall we say induction? . . . has to take place under certain specific conditions. One of those conditions is that it be an equinox—vernal or autumnal. I presume you're interested in vernal."

She was having trouble breathing. "Spring is two and a half months away!"

"So it is."

"You didn't tell me."

"You, my dear conjurer princess, didn't ask." He opened the book again.

She went and stood in his light and saw his eyes narrow in annoyance. "No, wait, please, just a moment," she begged.

"What is it?"

"This rite, ceremony, whatever . . . You'll do it *this* March?"

"Yes."

"Does it need to be done at a particular time of day?"

"Oh," he said, "midnight. Of course."

"Any special equipment?"

"I'll bring it." He was becoming dreadfully impatient, but she had to make sure there were no more surprises.

"Does any training come with this?"

"Afterwards. A day or so. Depending on how fast you learn."

She licked her lips nervously. "And then I'll be able to . . . you know, do the sort of things you do. . . ?"

Harkta threw his head back and laughed. "I very much doubt it." He grabbed her wrists before she could go for his eyes. "Everyone's different," he said, still laughing. "Some people are inclined to one thing, others to something else. Take healing, for instance. I can't do it at all. Some people take naturally to that, or to shape-changing, or to pyrotechnics. Most can't learn any magic worth a damn. There's no telling before you try, though." He tightened his hold on her wrists—though she hadn't moved, had been too shocked to move—intentionally hurting her. "Don't worry, little conjurer princess, you come through the equinox and I'll teach you magic. But don't even think of trying to leave. Wizards have ways of getting even with people who try to back out of contracts."

He shoved her away and said, "Clear the snow from the walk so my clients can get here easily. And when you're through with that, you can clean the cellar. That should keep you out from underfoot for a day or two."

The worst task was the one to which she had been looking forward. Help him with his magic, he had said.

People would come to him, asking for healing poultices, or love potions, or something to make an enemy's wife run away with somebody else. Lylene learned that there was nothing more than ground turnips and chunks of rosemary and laundry water that went into these mixtures, but if somebody complained that the spell didn't work, Harkta would tell them it was because they weren't pure of heart.

She would have suspected he didn't have any magic, except that she washed the front hall every day and sometimes it was rough gray fieldstones, and sometimes it was all polished marble and glass mirrors and flickering golden candles. And once in a while, bringing him his breakfast in the morning, she would catch Harkta still asleep, and she would find him a middle-aged man with too big a belly and not enough hair.

She discovered how he could know so much about her during that first meeting. Harkta paid people to bring him news, to tell him about what was going on in the town of Cragsfall, who was arguing with his neighbor, who was suffering from winter fevers, whether any strangers had come. Someone must have run all the way from the inn where she had stopped to ask directions, bringing Harkta word of the young woman seeking a wizard.

Now, when a woman came whose daughter had died, Harkta had Lylene hide in the next room and talk in a little voice, saying things that were either vague or common knowledge around Cragsfall. ("Remember when we went picking apples together? I miss you, Momma.") Another time she helped Harkta locate a lost breeding sow, an animal he had enticed out of its pen the night before.

But mostly he told futures. And since it was when he was doing this that the appearance of the front hall shifted, she suspected that here, finally, was something he really could do. It was this which kept her to their agreement, which kept her from leaving. This, and the knowledge that she had nowhere else to go.

Once a young man came, wringing his cap in his hands and asking Harkta to read his fortune. He left afterward, his face ashen, his hat forgotten, and Lylene said, "As long as you're going to cheat some poor fool out of his earnings, you could at least have given him good news." The more she knew him, the less she hoped for from the coming of the equinox.

"Lylene," Harkta said, putting his hands behind his neck, stretching, like a man whose muscles have stiffened from hours of hard work. "Lylene, my precious. I never cheat. Well, hardly ever. At least not as far as future-seeing goes."

"You cheat about everything."

Harkta laughed. "Well. But I *can* see into the future, and the future won't let me lie. It's all hard work. I hope you aren't under the misconception that magic will make everything easy for you. Maintaining this house, farseeing: That's hard work, you know."

Maintaining the house. Opening and closing doors. Lighting fires. How was any of this going to help win Beryl back? "If you can tell what's to be," she said, "then you could look to the vernal equinox and let me know what to expect."

Harkta caressed his moustache. "Oh, I would if I could, my dear. And since you've won such a special place in my heart with all your hard work, I'd do it for a bargain rate. But I'm afraid you're a blind spot for me, at least for the time being."

"Excuse me?"

He held up his hand. "How many fingers?"

She pulled back. "Two."

He moved the hand closer to her face. "No, don't back away." He held the fingers together, laying them against the tip of her nose. "How many?"

"Two."

"Stop being stubborn. How many do you *see*?"

The view jumped from one eye to the other until her eyes began to water. It could be anywhere from one to three. "I can't *see,*" she said, pushing his hand back. "You're too close."

"Exactly."

"Exactly what?"

"You're too close. For the time being." He touched the side of his brow. "My own future's a blind spot." He grinned. "Which means, of course, you're a part of my future." He raised his eyebrows and his grin became lecherous. "Perhaps you will grow up to be pretty after all. Perhaps you'll consider staying on after the equinox, and be my own little conjurer princess."

"I'm not a princess," she reminded for the twentieth or thirtieth time. "And you're a pig and a liar!"

He shrugged. "I can't lie about the future. It's the verbal equivalent to a blind spot." Again the grin. "Of course, you have no way of knowing if that's true."

5

The vernal equinox finally came.

Tomorrow, Lylene promised herself. She would be satisfied with whatever she could learn by tomorrow, and would not spend another night under Harkta's roof, for she mistrusted the way he'd been looking at her lately, as though he no longer considered her a child.

They needed a crossroads, the wizard said, and they set out after supper, walking in silence down the street, through the town, beyond the outlying farms. They passed several crossroads.

Harkta offered no explanations and Lylene didn't ask. Generally half of what he said could safely be ignored anyway, and after tonight she would know for herself.

The sun had set and a full moon had risen in the cloudless sky before Harkta spoke his first words since they had set out: "This will do."

The road that crossed the one they'd been

on—the Cragsfall to Arandell route—was overgrown, as though it hadn't been used in years. Lylene bent to look at the weather-grayed sign that had fallen among the weeds.

"Derrick's Crossing," Harkta said, nodding to the left as he emptied his satchel, "and that way: Fairhaven."

"Popular places." Candles, she saw. Harkta had brought nigh onto three score candles.

"Both gone now." Harkta stood in the center of the road, took five paces in the direction they had come, and plunked an unlit candle down in the road. "But I remember them well." He returned to the center, marked off a distance of five paces in the other direction with another candle. "Derrick's Crossing got plague one summer, probably brought in by the local priest who'd just come back from a pilgrimage. Then they got Vikings. No doubt blown off a course to better pickings. Big blond lack-wits. Come looking for gold, looking for women. In a place like Derrick's Crossing. By the time they caught on that the pit was for burning bodies, not garbage, they must have known it was too late. They burned the whole place down, people and all, then set off in their dragon boat. If they had any sense at all, they sank it under them before they reached the sea." The wizard took five paces toward Derrick's Crossing and put a candle down.

Lylene rubbed her arms. Now that they were no longer walking, the night seemed chill.

"This way, here, this was the shortcut to the mill. Can't see the path anymore, but it used to go between those two trees there. Nice family, the people that ran it. Priest I was telling you about, he went to visit them right after getting back from the Holy Land so that he could baptize the daughter they'd had while he'd been away." He yanked out a handful of grass, set a candle in the indentation that was left. "Now Fairhaven—ah, Fairhaven. That's a different story entirely."

"I don't want to hear it."

The wizard shrugged.

"Anyway, there hasn't been plague—or Vikings—around here in at least fifty years."

Harkta paused, considering. "That's just about right," he said.

Lylene looked away skeptically.

"I'm older than I look."

It was his standard answer whenever she caught him trying to pull something over on her: You're ignorant and know nothing about magic, if the issue was of a supernatural nature; I'm older than I look, to cover anything else. She indicated the moon. "Let's just—"

"These things can't be rushed. You don't know anything about magic, so stop pushing me. Stand here." He had set out five candles, one for each of the diverging paths, and now moved her to a spot near the center. Next he pulled his sword from its scabbard and used it to scratch a circle into the ground within the perimeter of the candles.

With the remaining candles, the wizard formed a five-pointed star within the circle, its points aimed at the spaces between the original five candles. He had her stand in the exact center of the star. "Kneel, princess."

Lylene had forgotten all about being cold.

Harkta knelt in front of her and used the sword to loosen a clump of dirt which he then crumbled and put in a pouch at his belt. He took the last item from his satchel, a clear flask which contained clear liquid, removed the stopper, and put the flask in a second pouch. "It's just water," he told her. "Don't be startled. Once it starts, stand when I stand, speak only when I indicate you're to speak."

She nodded, then finally found her voice: "Once it starts?"

"Now we wait for midnight, exactly."

Lylene glanced at the sky.

"I will know," he answered her unasked question. He knelt with the sword across his knees, his hands upraised at shoulder level, his face tipped upward.

I will know, Lylene thought. *What pretentious nonsense!* She gazed at her hands folded in her lap because it made her uncomfortable to watch the wizard's face, drained of color, of movement, of anything human, staring at the stars. She had just enough time to grow impatient when she felt a touch: the merest brush of a fingernail perhaps, at the base of her neck, under her hair, where no one could possibly get, then up, up, almost past feeling, onto her scalp.

At the same moment, Harkta bowed his head, sketched graceful twin circles in the air with his hands, then let his hands drop to the sword—the left at the jeweled hilt, the right at the tip. He raised the sword over his head and stood, so suddenly that Lylene had to scramble to keep up.

He planted his feet firmly apart, holding the sword as though offering it to the heavens, and spoke in a loud and firm voice. "By the power of air," he said, and as though in response, a breeze came out from the dark stillness, lifting her damp hair from her damp face. The wizard was still speaking: ". . . and earth . . ."—he let go the tip of the sword, reached into the first pouch, then traced a gritty star on her forehead— ". . . and water . . ."—he reached into the flask, sprinkled her face, then took hold of the swordtip again—". . . and fire . . ."—the five outermost candles flickered into flame—". . . I summon thee. When the bright hours of day equal the long minutes of night, when the time is neither day nor night, when the place is neither here nor there, from the in-between times, from the in-between places—come to us."

At the first touch of the breeze the crawly sensation spread from Lylene's neck and head to her entire body.

Nothing—nothing—stirred in the night.

Harkta stretched his arms higher, spoke in a louder voice: "By the power of air . . ." Inside their circle, the wind spun last year's leaves around their legs. ". . . and earth . . . and water . . ."—Harkta's hands remained on the upraised sword, but Lylene's face tingled everywhere he had touched her with earth and water—"and fire . . ."—the candles that formed the outline of the star in which they stood blazed upward, preternaturally high—". . . I summon thee. By the seven orders of angels, by the six fingers of Satan's left hand, by the five points on this star, by the four primal elements, by our three summonings, by the two of us, by the one Power—come to us."

The wind . . . the moonlight on the sword . . . Harkta's voice . . . Lylene held her breath, waiting.

Harkta nodded at her. "We summon thee . . ." he intoned, then waited for her.

"We summon thee," she repeated shakily. *I'm coming, Beryl,* she thought.

". . . by the power of air . . ."

This time, no reaction.

Till she said it: ". . . by the power of air . . ." The blast of wind nearly knocked her down, but she kept her feet firmly in the center of the star, as he had told her to.

". . . and earth . . ." Harkta was shouting to be heard over the howling gale.

". . . and earth . . ."

The tingle where he had touched her brow began to burn.

". . . and water . . ." There was a wild exuberance in his voice. He was in his glory, Lylene could tell: The power, the danger, the drama—he was loving every bit of it.

She repeated, though she knew the burning would spread to wherever the water had touched her face: ". . . and water . . ."

His voice had a final, triumphant ring to it. ". . . and fire!"

". . . and fire!"

The flames burst from within her, exploded down onto her, were her, as she was them. She threw her hands in front of her face to protect her eyes from the shimmering glare. She opened her mouth to scream, sucked in fire that seared her nose, throat, chest. Screaming, fire came from her mouth, then got pulled in again with the next inhaling. And still she breathed: She was alive, not dead, not dying, alive.

Her head spun, sparkles of color like bursting

blossoms pricked her closed eyelids, noises crackled and hissed and chittered within her ears. She could still smell the fire, not the scent of something burning but the flames themselves, and she felt the pleasant, unbearable heat on her body, even though she realized her body was no longer there.

Her senses had no words for what she experienced, and she couldn't hold on to it. She felt the memory slipping, already—escaping, irretrievable, like womb-dreams, like water through fingers.

There were voices, and of all things they spoke of what Harkta had spoken of: names and Names. They spoke of making things, of destroying, of illusion. Some of the voices she almost remembered, from a time before memory; some almost solidified into shapes. At times they seemed heartbreakingly clear—pure and beautiful; other times she was sure it was demons to whom she listened. But: No evil, they whispered to her just before they faded away the last time, no good, only . . . only . . . She missed the last word.

Again her body was burning. But this time it was different. It was the sensation of a leg too long sat upon—all prickles and heat. And the more she thought about it, the more she thought that now she had a body again, and it was lying down. Yes, she was sure of it. Face down. On the ground. She smelled earth and grass, felt dampness that may have been dew underneath her and warmth that may have been sunshine on her back.

She was left with one strong memory: seeing herself put her hands on either side of an object, and that object doubled. It was a simple matter of concentration. But meanwhile . . .

"Harkta," she said, "get your hands off me."

Her voice creaked, rasped like an old woman's. She opened her eyes.

Early morning. Harkta was crouched next to her, grinning. He made a show of lifting his hands away, then stood and backed off.

Her hair was all tangled around her face and arms, suffocating her. The prickling sensation had gone, but she was all aches and pains. She blinked to clear the film from her eyes. Everything else looked fine, but the mass of hair lying across her shoulders and arms was out of focus. (She remembered the wizard holding two fingers up to her nose.) But would being too close account for the lack of color? It looked palest silver, an old woman's hair to go with the old woman's voice. *Something's not right,* she thought, even before she lifted her hand to brush the hair out of her eyes, even before she saw the distended veins, the brown spots of age, the cracks and wrinkles.

She tried to jump up, gasped at sharp pains

in her back and legs. Pains not of exposure, but of age.

Harkta leaned over to hold her elbow, to support her.

She beat his hands away. "What did you do to me?" Her accusing scream came out a petulant whimper.

"I did nothing," the wizard said. "These things take a lot out of you."

She looked at her hands and couldn't tell if they were shaking from palsy or agitation. "How long?" she demanded. "How long?"

"How long have you lain here? One night: seven or eight hours. No extraordinary amount of time has passed, if that's what you mean. Near as I can guess, time between the astral planes passes at a faster rate than it does here—speeds up the body processes. If you mean how long does it *look* like you've lost . . ." He shrugged. "I'd say you look . . . seventy."

"*Seventy?* Why didn't you tell me this would happen?"

"The right moment to approach the subject never came up."

"Damn you!" She tried to rise but made it only as far as her hands and knees. Harkta had more than enough time to back out of range. "You beast! You miserable . . . treacherous . . ." She started to cry because she didn't even have the vocabulary to tell him what she thought of him.

"Oh come now," the wizard said. "Stop making such a fuss. You're taking this quite badly, don't you think?" He fidgeted at the periphery of her arms' reach. "See. You don't listen. It's not as though it's forever." He indicated himself.

Lylene gulped. Once. Twice. Whispered: "You mean it'll go away?"

The wizard pursed his lips. "Well. Not exactly 'go away' as such . . ."

"What—exactly?"

"It's part of your new-found magical ability."

"I . . . *wish* it away?"

Harkta grinned. "There," he said expansively. "Yes. Now you've got it."

"I'm wishing it away now."

"Well, yes, but . . . Someone's got to be there. With your hands on him." He was well back of her now.

"I can get young again by making someone else old?"

The wizard nodded. "All at once, or a little bit at a time. You can divide it how you will."

By making someone else old?

The wizard sighed at her reaction. "Yes. Well. And it works with natural aging as well. Be careful and you may live forever. Somehow I get the feeling you're not the sort to be careful. But now you know. Any other questions?"

"I hate you."

"I said: Any other questions?"

Lylene reached into her mind, into the experience she had just been through, for which she had lived the past several weeks, and tried to find something with which to hurt the wizard. She couldn't make fire, she hadn't the ability to weave illusions, and the future was beyond her. Duplication. That, too, was a matter of wishing, of concentrating. But what a niggardly power for such an awful price! How could that help her with the wizard? How could that help her with Beryl?

"Well, if that's it, then . . ." Harkta said. "I'll be willing to take you back, once you're presentable. . . . You might consider stopping at seventeen or eighteen. That's much nicer than sixteen." He smoothed his moustache, shouldered the satchel, and started walking back the way they had come, toward Cragsfall.

He knows, Lylene thought: He had to know. He was aware of what had passed and of the extent of her magic. If he had seen her endowed with an ability that surpassed his own, he would have beat a hasty retreat while she slept. Or killed her. Or killed her, she realized.

She pushed herself up to her feet. "Does it work with animals?" she called after him. "Can I pass my years off onto an animal?"

Harkta stopped, turned. "I have no idea." He resumed walking.

She forced her reedy voice into a shout, asked the question she had never thought to ask before: "How old *are* you?"

Harkta looked over his shoulder. "Lessons are over, little one," he laughed. "Our contract's fulfilled."

Lylene shouted at his retreating back, "How old's your cook?"

The breeze carried his laugh to her, but he didn't turn back again.

6

She headed away from Cragsfall, toward the city of Arandell. If she kept moving, she wouldn't have to think.

By nightfall she had made it only as far as one of the outlying villages. The people there told her that another hour would get her to the city, but that the gates would be closed by then. Lylene knew she couldn't have made it if the city were on the other side of the village common. She sat down heavily on the ground.

The villagers stood off to the side, watching her warily. Here she was, with hair as white as the oldest of them, dressed in good-quality clothes except that her dress hung on her shrunken frame, exposing more of her than would have been seemly but because she was so wrinkled and shriveled she appeared more ludicrous than lewd. In the end, they must have decided she looked too pitiful to be dangerous, for they offered her the use of the village byre to spend the night.

With the wind rattling the daub and wattle walls and starlight showing through the badly mended thatch, Lylene knelt in the fresh-smelling straw and studied the two cows with which she shared shelter. They looked as old as she felt, as they stood there chewing, chewing, and watching her. "Easy," she murmured, "easy. I won't hurt you." Gingerly, knowing that the villagers' livelihood depended on these animals, Lylene wished away a year or two.

She felt nothing.

If the cow felt anything, it didn't indicate so.

Lylene wished away more years. Still she saw no change. She concentrated as hard as she could and wished she were sixteen going on seventeen again.

The cow flicked its tail and kept on chewing, oblivious to her now.

So. It didn't work with animals.

Now to try the other . . . She removed her cloak and held it in her wrinkled hands. Concentrated on that. A shiver started in her chest. A flash of light inside her head. And Lylene held two identical cloaks. It gave her a grim sense of satisfaction: She was old, she was friendless, she was no closer to rescuing Beryl than she had been that afternoon in Castle Delroy's garden—how many lifetimes ago?—but at least she wouldn't be cold.

She wrapped herself in both cloaks and went to sleep.

She woke when the villagers came to let out the cows in the morning. A group of children were gathered around, watching her.

Stiffly, she sat up. When she stood, the children scattered. She shook the straw out of her cloak—and realized there *was* only one.

Lylene went outside, hobbling from a dull pain in her hip. "Where's my cloak?" she demanded of the villagers. "Who stole my cloak?" The idea that someone had been able to sneak in, had watched her while she slept all unaware—this was more upsetting than the loss of something she now knew she could replace with little effort.

"It's on your back," someone muttered.

There was snickering. Because she was a crazy old woman? Or because they knew where it was? "The other one," she said, knowing the innocents in the crowd—if there were any—would have no idea what she was talking about.

They looked at her with blank faces. No

telling which. She took the hand of the man who had spoken, holding it in both hers. "Thanks for all your kindness," she said, wishing a year onto him. She felt a slight tingle.

"Yeah, right," the man said, pulling his hand away.

Lylene reached for another hand, the woman who had suggested that she stay in the byre. "You've been so kind," she murmured. Again the tingle.

The woman nodded, saying nothing.

"And you," Lylene grabbed at another hand, no matter which, and another, and another. "So kind. Thank you for your hospitality to an old woman. Thank you." She shook their hands, to distract them from the strange tingling. It must be beginning to show, she thought, after several long moments of it. Not on any of them, but she had just dropped more than a dozen years, and they were beginning to look askance at her.

"Good-bye," she said, backing away from them, edging toward the road to Arandell. They continued to stare at her, nobody saying anything, nobody making a move to stop her. She started down the road but turned, uneasy with them at her back. No one was following. She forced a jaunty wave. Several times more she checked and always found them still gathered at the edge of the village, until a curve took them from her sight.

What had she done? she thought.

And what had she become?

Lylene reached Arandell about mid-morning.

It was a big place, crowded, and with an incredible number of shops and stalls selling everything imaginable. Vendors hailed her, encouraging her to step closer: to try their savory-smelling meat pies, to look, to touch—"Go ahead, touch!"—leather goods, worked metal, satin ribbons, tiny carved wood saints. Black and white shaggy goats bleated in their stalls. The breeze flapped the canvas tents, set to tinkling the glass beads one merchant had hanging on a wooden rack. For the first time in her life she saw slaves being sold.

She had paused before approaching the city gates to make another duplicate cloak, and now she sold this so that she would have money for lodgings. It was a bad bargain—the merchant could see her desperation—and Lylene knew it. She leaned over the counter to shake his hand.

She doubled the money he gave her and put some of it in her belt pouch, used some to buy a steaming mince pie. The woman charged a reasonable amount, and Lylene didn't shake her hand.

Next she found a stall that specialized in blades, old and new: knives, axes, swords. The proprietor was a burly man with a sun-darkened, scarred face that made him look more a soldier than a merchant. *That's what I need,* she thought: *soldiers.* How much, she wondered, to buy an army? When she asked him where she should go to find some men for hire, he looked her up and down and gave a lewd laugh that earned him a hearty handshake. But he gave her a name—the Happy Wench Inn—and told her that come evening she could find a man there for any job.

"Happy Wench?" Lylene repeated, suspecting he was making fun of her, sending her to a whorehouse.

The blade merchant wiggled his eyebrows at her suggestively, which was not promising. But when she stopped and asked someone else, she was assured there really was such a place and it really was an inn.

Lylene hesitated again outside of the place. The painted sign that hung over the door was of a woman with a big bosom and a small dress, but she *was* holding two mugs overflowing with beer.

Truth be told, Lylene knew she wouldn't know a whorehouse if she saw one.

"Is this a tavern?" she asked a woman who was walking past.

The woman gave both Lylene and the place a disapproving glance, but nodded.

As soon as Lylene stepped into the public room of the inn, her head began to whirl—the barrels for tables, the smell of sawdust, the other patrons. Not honest shopkeepers or farmers by the look of them. She doubted that even here in Arandell did honest men have such scowling looks or knives tucked so ostentatiously in their belts. Still, no one was paying any attention to her. Apparently there was an advantage to appearing more than fifty years old, after all.

"I'm interested in a room," she told the surly-looking young man behind the serving counter. She'd rest until evening, then see about hiring some men to rescue Beryl from Theron. She handed the barkeep a gold piece. She had smaller, but she wanted to see the expression on his face when he had to make change.

He led her up a flight of stairs and opened a door for her, where he made a flourish with his hand and bowed. "Anything else, my lady?"

She closed the door without answering. The room was small but surprisingly clean. There was a bed, a stool, and a small table. She moved the table to block the door. Then she sat on the bed, wrapped her cloak around her, and leaned her back into the corner so that she faced the door, lest anybody tried to get in.

7

She woke up confused, unable to remember where this moonlit room was or what she was doing in it, all stiff and sore and cold.

Lylene reached to pull her cloak back up around her shoulders and couldn't find it. She stood up, patted the bed, still couldn't find it.

Unease crawled over her body. The table was still up against the door—nobody could have entered that way. But she hadn't thought to shutter the window.

She thought of it now, seeing the nearby roofs. A thief would have had no trouble getting up here while she slept. *Stupid!* she chided herself at the thought of someone leaning over her, silently deliberating whether to rob her, kill her, or rape her.

Lylene closed her eyes until the shaking went away. Nothing had come of it, she reassured herself, nobody had touched her. And in searching for the cloak she had felt her coins on the bed. They were still there. Fewer than there had been; but as long as she had any she had an unlimited supply.

She ripped a strip from her dress's hem to bind her hair back from her face. With the years she had wished away handshake by handshake, her hair had gone from pure white to grayish red—very unbecoming. Only another three dozen or so touches and she would be back where she started.

If she didn't keep making stupid mistakes.

She took a deep breath, moved the table away from the door, and went to the head of the stairs.

The public room, so nearly deserted this morning, was crowded. The place smelled of many bodies, of ale and roasting mutton. There were many weapons, some armor—metal as well as leather—and a good deal of loud talking. The Happy Wench clientele looked like mercenaries and thieves, every one of them. She made it halfway down the stairs when the barkeep from earlier in the day burst in from the back room. He started for the stairs, then stopped, seeing her. "You," he yelled.

What now?

"Where is it?" the man demanded.

"Where is what?" She had a question of her own for him, about the security of the place and how a cloak could disappear from someone's room, off someone's very back. But before she had a chance to complain, he yanked her the rest of the way down the stairs. "What the hell are you trying to get away with?" he demanded.

"What?" She glanced at the night bartender behind the counter, who watched but said nothing. As did several others. She hoped she appeared calmer than she felt. "What are you talking about? Stop pushing me."

"The money you gave me, woman. What d'ya do with it?"

Someone interrupted—"What are you talking about, Marsh?"—someone who was standing at the bar, involved because the disturbance kept him waiting for his drink.

"She gave me money this afternoon for a room, and now the money's gone."

"Seems to me that's your problem, Marsh," the night man said, "not hers. It's your responsibility to keep track of what you take in."

"But I had it," the man called Marsh said, shoving his face close to Lylene's. "A gold piece. Fancy money for an old hag who don't belong in a place like this to begin with. I kept it in my pocket all afternoon, then I laid it on the table when I was counting up just now. I was looking right at it, and it just faded away."

"Gave it to Lena, more like," someone called, "for what Lena does best."

One of the serving girls tossed her hair. "Not me!" she exclaimed, hand on hip.

"Or lost it," the night man interrupted. "I told you, Marsh, that's your responsibility."

But Lylene felt a cold, hard spot in her stomach. She remembered the cloak that had disappeared last night, and the second one today. She tried to think back and realized the duplicates had always appeared to the right. She *had* sold the original and kept the duplicate, just as she had given the barkeep the duplicate gold piece. The cold spot enveloped her entire body. Her magic didn't have staying power. The things she made wouldn't last out the day.

And hard on that she thought of the villagers—and how she had repaid their hospitality.

"Witchcraft," Marsh said, glaring, knowing that he spoke the truth about the missing money, and knowing that she knew. "This old woman gave me enchanted money."

Somebody gave him a good-natured shove, which he returned with less good nature.

Lylene eased around him. This had been a bad idea all along. She had thought a strong man or two—or twenty or thirty—could take on Theron and his armed fortress at Saldemar. But even if that plan would work—and at this point she was no longer sure it would—certainly this was not the place to find trustworthy employees.

Lylene kept moving but glanced back. A ruddy-faced man with a blond beard was talking earnestly with the two bartenders. Someone from the village of the night before? There was no way to be certain. And even if he were, what could he possibly say against her?

Still, she kept watching them, rather than where she was going, and bumped someone's arm, spilling a drink and getting soundly cursed.

And re-attracted Marsh's attention.

She apologized profusely, but the man with the wet sleeve kept on and on, and in a moment Marsh loomed in front of her. "I want to talk to you," he said, loud enough to attract the attention of anyone who wasn't listening already.

Lylene shrank back. "I've done nothing wrong."

"I want to see your money."

"I already paid you once."

"I want to see your money."

She took another step away and felt the wall at her back. "I'm here with friends," she lied. "You'd better leave me alone."

The man snorted. "Who're you with, witch?"

Lylene glanced around the room. Cutthroats and thieves. Which, of course, was what—until a moment ago—she had been looking for. Several watched her with eager leers and shining eyes at least as dangerous as what she already faced.

"Come on, witch, who you with?"

She dragged her gaze back across the room, searching for someone who might help her and not cut her throat afterward. She stopped at a table with two men: one probably not yet thirty years old and dark haired, the other slightly younger and blond. The one with the fair hair stood out, in this room of knives and swords, as being heavily armed. He was one of the few who was uninterested by the situation in the room and instead faced the door, watching whatever was going on outside the ale house. His companion, on the other hand, sat with his elbows on the table, chin resting on his fists, watching her. Once he caught her eye, he raised his brows, then glanced at the empty stool at their table.

"You're coming with me." Marsh reached for her.

Lylene dodged. "Them," she said. "I'm with them."

The burly barkeep turned to look, and Lylene slipped past him, rushing to the table, where she hurriedly sat.

Her benefactor smiled at her—a smile that seemed kind and gentle yet indicated he would fight like the devil to protect her. Or at least that was what she hoped the smile told her. He winked—but he seemed to be shrinking even as she watched. In truth, he was sliding down off his stool, slowly, slowly, until his knees were on the floor and the edge of his chin hit the edge of the table.

Lylene grabbed his arm just before he disappeared under the table and hauled him back into his seat.

He smiled and nodded in acknowledgement, then gradually dropped forward, with his face in the spilled ale on the table, and began to snore.

Lylene swallowed hard, took a deep breath, and sat back down, facing the second man, the fair-haired one.

At least she had his attention now. He looked at her coldly. No telling how sober he was—nor what he was thinking—from that expression.

"She with you?" Marsh called across the room.

Her table companion looked up, perhaps evaluating the speaker as he had—perhaps—evaluated her.

Lylene stole a glance at the man asleep on the table. Dark, curly hair and a swarthy complexion. He might have been a Greek—as his friend, with his long flaxen hair, may have been a Norseman. She wouldn't put it past her luck to have chosen as rescuers two foreigners who didn't speak the language.

The possible Viking was watching her again, his blue eyes still cold and unfathomable, even as Marsh stopped at their table and repeated, "She with you?"

The steady gaze didn't shift from her. "Yes," the young man said, no trace of an accent after all. "She's with us."

Marsh considered for a moment, then grabbed Lylene by the arm anyway.

The blond man caught hold of the barkeep's wrist.

"All right, all right. She's with you." Marsh let go of Lylene and was released in turn. He readjusted his shirt, glared at Lylene without looking at either of the men at her table, and headed back to his friends, ignoring the snickers and catcalls from the inn's other occupants.

"Thank you," Lylene said.

The young man—mercenary, she was sure of it—sat back with that appraising look still on his face.

Lylene lowered her gaze to her clasped hands and wondered how one went about hiring mercenaries.

The conversation around the room resumed. When she looked up again, the mercenary still faced her but was obviously focused on a point somewhere beyond her left shoulder. She turned and saw Marsh and his friends gathered near the bar, their heads close together. "If you see me safely out of town," she whispered, "I'll pay you."

"How much?"

Lylene pulled her last silver piece and two coppers out of her money purse and set them on the table.

The mercenary folded his arms across his chest and looked at her skeptically.

Lylene untied the purse so that the entire contents spilled onto the table: two more smaller copper pieces, several tin.

He sighed, as though not used to selling himself so cheap, then swept up the money. And continued to sit.

"Should we leave?" she asked testily.

"Eventually." He finished his drink while she thought she'd die of the strain. Then he ordered another.

Lylene watched the serving girl approach, smiling and swinging her hips. The girl leaned over the blond mercenary to give him his fresh drink, then moved round to the other side of the table to lean way low while mopping up the spilled ale around their sleeping companion's face, living up to the establishment's sign. The third time she ran the cold wet cloth over Lylene's hand because she was too busy showing off her bosom to notice what she was doing, Lylene said, "I really don't think we need you any more."

"Maybe *you* don't," the girl said, blowing a parting kiss to Lylene's mercenary.

Lylene felt her face go red. Here she'd just handed over all her money to this man so that he would protect her, and he was spending that money on beer, flirting with the serving girls, and looking at her frustration in open amusement. "Plan on drinking yourself into a drunken stupor?" she snapped.

"No."

"That's probably what your friend thought, before he fell face first into the table."

"Ah, but it was Shile's turn," he answered, as though that explained anything.

She wondered what he'd say if she demanded her money returned, then wondered what the rest of the room would say if she tried to leave alone. She turned around in her seat. Marsh was still there, as were his friends. Lylene waited.

The man she'd employed had just finished his drink—and he had taken a very long time at it—when three heavily armed men came in wearing unmatched pieces of armor, equipment scavenged from the field. Nothing out of the ordinary, not here. Except that her Viking friend was watching them.

"What—" she started, but he cut her off with a whispered profanity. Lylene whirled around. One of the just-entered men and Marsh were greeting each other like long-lost brothers.

"Turn around!" her companion commanded her between clenched teeth. He nudged his friend under the table with his foot, hissing, "Shile."

The dark-haired man raised his head a handspan off the table. He saw Lylene, and his face softened into a smile. "S'alright, I'll take care of you," he said, then sprawled across the table again.

His associate kicked him more roughly than before. "Shile!"

The older man opened his eyes, his face still on the table. "What?"

"Can you walk?"

"S'e here?"

"Your sure thing never showed."

"Ah, well," Shile said philosophically. Then: "We in trouble, Weiland?"

His friend, looking beyond him, nodded.

"Just give me a moment."

The one called Weiland moved his head slightly, an indication that there wasn't a moment to give.

"Right," Shile said without moving.

Weiland stood up abruptly, knocking his stool out of the way.

Lylene kicked back her stool, stood and turned in the same movement. Six men, including the three newcomers and the barkeep who had started all this, were closing in on them, so that now only one table separated them. But Marsh was bent over double, and one of the others had a very strange expression on his face. Lylene saw that before she saw the knife handle sticking out of his throat, right above where the chain mail started.

Weiland was holding another knife—this one pulled from its hiding place in the leather bracer around his left wrist. His third shot went wide, bouncing harmlessly off chain mail. Marsh lay motionless on the floor, a red puddle forming beneath him.

Swords scraped against scabbards. Chairs and tables scratched across the floor as some, who had found themselves too close, scrambled out of range, while others, who wanted to be a part of the coming melee, moved in.

Shile was still sprawled across their table. Weiland had pulled an incredibly long sword from its place at his back but now grabbed Lylene's arm with his left hand and started for the door, abandoning his own partner. "But . . ." Lylene protested.

Weiland jerked on her arm as he countered a sword thrust from someone blocking the way, then slashed across that man's chest before moving against another whose weapon was still half-sheathed.

There was a shout and a crash from behind. Lylene turned. At the last, Shile hadn't been as drunk as his posture had indicated: He had flung the remains of his drink into the face of one of Marsh's friends, then tipped the table over onto several other men.

Watching him, she stumbled, jerking on Weiland's arm as two swordsmen closed in. Weiland yanked her to her feet, cursing, then let go as the two men separated, coming at him from either side. He lunged at the one on his left, but the man danced back, just out of range. Weiland whipped back in time to parry a blow from the other and had enough power behind the stroke to stagger the man a few paces backward. But he wasn't able to press his advantage; he had to face left again.

This time the man on the left pressed in, battling blow for blow so that Weiland couldn't turn away for an instant. Couldn't defend his back. Couldn't see the right-hand man raise his sword.

Lylene kicked the back of that one's knee.

The man's leg buckled, and he hit the floor.

Weiland thrust into the first man's stomach, then whirled around, killing the second man before he could retrieve his fallen sword.

Lylene's hands flew to cover her mouth, and she took a step away. Someone grabbed her from behind. Steadied her. Then started pushing her forward. "Move!" It was Shile shouting into her ear.

Weiland cleared a way to the door; Shile covered their backs. But by the time they got to the door, there was no more opposition.

At the far end of the common room, some of those who hadn't gotten involved, or who had taken themselves out of the fracas early, had seated themselves at unturned tables, as though nothing out of the ordinary had happened. Others made their way back to that area of calm, hugging to the walls to keep out of harm's way. A few scattered into the darkness outside. The night man peeked out from behind the counter. "All right, all right," he said, trying to sound in control, "break it up now. Excitement's over."

Shile pushed Lylene out through the open door, into the clean outside air.

8

"You killed those men," Lylene protested. "Some of them didn't have their swords out." Even Randal, despite his tendency to be a bully, had believed in chivalry and wouldn't have cut down an unarmed man.

Weiland swore and set off down the street.

Shile took hold of her arm and made to catch up. "Weiland, slow down."

Weiland paused only long enough to wipe his blade clean on his breeches leg before slipping the sword into its sheath. Dark stains on clothing were less likely to draw attention than a naked blade.

"Weiland." Shile let go of Lylene's arm to catch up to his taller friend's long-legged stride.

Weiland turned an instant before Shile reached him. "We have to assume some of those people had friends," he said.

"Aye," Shile agreed tiredly. He sheathed his own unbloodied sword. "Best we left town."

Weiland nodded beyond him. "Someone's coming."

Lylene whipped around, hearing footsteps approach from around the corner they had just passed. "It's only a lone townsman," she hissed, hoping for no more bloodshed.

Weiland and Shile put themselves between her and the corner. Neither had drawn a weapon. Yet.

The townsman gave a startled glance at the three of them blocking his way. He put his hand to his side, where he may have kept his money, or a knife.

Didn't he have eyes to see? Perhaps he too had come from an alehouse and that was where he got the courage to stand up to what her companions obviously were.

And with that thought of alehouses and companions, Lylene began to sing. It was an old drinking round, one that her father had used to sing—much to her mother's chagrin. She couldn't remember half the words, and probably half of what she thought she remembered was wrong, but inaccuracy wouldn't hurt her credibility. Nothing odd, nothing to fear in an old drunken woman.

All three of the men looked at her as though she were mad.

It was Shile who caught on first. Moving backward, he tripped on a cobblestone, and only Weiland's intervention kept him on his feet. "Thank you," Shile said, loudly and tipsily. "Thank you very mush. So kind." He staggered, almost fell, almost brought Weiland down with him. "So nice to have good friends when one is indis . . . indis . . . indisposed." He came close to falling on the townsman, who watched him with growing distaste. "Isen it?" Shile insisted, putting a friendly arm around him. The man leaned as far away from him as he could get. "Isen it nice to have friends?"

"Shile. Come on, Shile." Weiland disentangled the two men. "Sorry," he said to the other, who, seeing they were harmless after all, was beginning to look annoyed. "Shile!"

"S'nice," Shile insisted. "Is."

The man shoved past him but stopped short of pushing Weiland, who was considerably taller and not quite so unsteady on his feet. He scurried around Lylene, as though afraid she, too, might try talking to him.

Shile gave a deep bow, his hand nearly brushing the street.

Weiland whacked Shile on the arm to get him moving. Each grabbed one of Lylene's arms, and they took off in the opposite direction from the townsman.

"Good thinking!" Shile told her.

Before she could ask what the hurry was, they made a quick left turn, then a right; they scrambled over a wooden fence that blocked off an alley, squeezed between two shops closed for the night, made another left, then another, and finally entered an inn, though one with more ordinary-looking folk in it than at the Happy Wench.

But she had time for no more than that quick observation as they crossed the public room at a half-run; then they were in the back wing, where the sleeping accommodations were.

This was all going too fast. Lylene stiffened, ready to dig her feet into the wooden planking, but Shile skidded to a halt, and Weiland let go and pulled out his sword.

Shile moved her against the wall and motioned her to silence.

Weiland raised his foot and kicked in the door. Lylene heard the wood splinter—*crack*—as it slammed against the wall.

Apparently there was nothing amiss.

Weiland sheathed his sword as Shile pulled her into the room, then Weiland kicked what was left of the door shut behind them. While Shile threw open the shutters to give them light to see by, Weiland took a money purse he hadn't had earlier when she had paid him, and he dumped the contents on the bed to count it.

Lylene remembered him separating the townsman from Shile, Shile who had so readily played the drunk—to avoid a confrontation, she had assumed. "You do this often," she asked, "these cut and run tactics?"

"My Lady!" It was Shile who pocketed the money. "Only in desperate times. Under less hectic conditions, Weiland and I are what you might call master locksmiths." Weiland, gathering their belongings, gave a sharp look. Shile shrugged. "Of sorts."

A timid knock sounded on the door—politeness, for the door sagged, a wide gap between it and the frame. "Excuse me . . ." A balding man who had to be the proprietor peeked in, wiping his hands nervously on his apron. "Excuse me, is there some sort of trouble?"

Weiland had pulled a knife from his pack. He slipped it into his wrist bracer to replace one of those lost at the Happy Wench.

The owner nervously wet his lips, as Weiland got another knife and fitted it to the harness which held his sword.

"No trouble," Shile said. He held out several copper pieces. The owner finally tore his gaze from Weiland. "We'll need our horses readied. We're leaving right away."

Which was what the man no doubt wanted to hear. He took the money and fled.

"Now," Shile said, "my Lady . . . ?"

"Lylene."

"That's a pretty name."

She didn't know how to answer that, from a man such as this, in a situation such as this.

"Will you be joining us?"

"The *Lady,*"—Weiland's tone indicated he thought she was no such thing—"has paid us to get her out of town." He got yet another knife and hid it in his boot.

"Which road?"

"Any road."

Shile raised his eyebrows. "That's . . . rather vague."

Lylene cut in. "That was all I had the money to afford."

"That was more," Weiland said, "than you had the money to afford."

"Now, now." Shile smiled at both of them. He had never quite lost his dazed, half-drunk look, but he was gentle as he took Lylene's hand in both of his. "You're in some sort of trouble, I can tell. And that's what Weiland and I do best: We help ladies in trouble."

Weiland leaned against the door, holding it open for them. Lylene looked from one to the other and evaluated them against Harkta. "I have no money."

"Well,"—Shile smiled equably—"that's always a disappointment, but we won't worry about it just now."

Lylene considered the two men and put

things together. "You heard the innkeeper talking about that gold piece that disappeared."

Perhaps Shile considered denying it. He took a deep breath, but in the end only said, "Yes."

"Disappearing money," Weiland said to him. "Sounds like just what we need."

"But fascinating. It does sound fascinating. Look,"—he turned to Lylene—"you already paid Weiland for us to escort you out of Arandell. . . ." What he had just said seemed to suddenly catch up with him. He turned to Weiland. "Did she pay you in gold?"

Weiland winced.

She glanced from one to the other. That was all she needed. "The money I gave you was good. Truly it was."

Shile looked more convinced than Weiland. He answered, "Then all that leaves is for you to decide: Will you join us or not? You've already paid us."

Which meant no refunds. Things had been simpler at Castle Delroy, where decisions were made for her. Now here was Shile with his trust-me look and Weiland with his I-hope-she-says-no look, and who was to say they were any different from Harkta or Theron or the men back at the Happy Wench? Yet Shile trusted her, that the money she had paid them to risk their lives was real. And that trust seemed to demand a certain amount of trust in return. "I need to get out of here," she admitted.

Shile took her arm. The three of them went out the back way, then circled round to the stable, avoiding the public room. The heavy set owner was seeing to the horses himself, one chestnut-colored, the other a magnificent bay. Destriers, the two of them: very fine, very expensive. Knight's war horses, though Shile and Weiland were obviously not knights. Weiland went to see to the bay, to check the saddling, to adjust the girth.

"We don't want any trouble," the owner said, back to that again.

And Shile, looking over his own horse, again said, "No trouble," and handed the man more money.

They fastened their kits to the saddles, then set out, Lylene riding with Shile. "Anything you need to go back to the Happy Wench for?" he asked.

She shook her head and tightened her grip around his waist as he kicked the horse into a full gallop.

Although neither man wore armor, destriers were bred big to carry a fully clad knight. The few people they saw scrambled out of the way as Lylene and her two companions tore through the streets.

They left by the north gate—the gate warden convinced to let them through by more of the money Lylene had unwittingly helped them steal from the passerby.

9

They set up camp still short of dawn. The men weighed the chill of the air against the likelihood of pursuit and finally built a fire, albeit a small one. They had strips of smoked venison and loaves of hard bread packed among their provisions. So, Lylene estimated, hasty departures were nothing new to them.

It was Shile who pointed out that there was a quantity of dried blood on the hem of Lylene's dress. Holding out a shirt and a pair of breeches, he said, "If you think you'd be more comfortable in men's clothing than . . . you know . . ."

Shile went to help Weiland rub down the horses while Lylene retreated out of the campfire's glow and with shaking hands pulled the breeches on under her dress. Shile's, she thought; Weiland's would have been much too long.

Once changed, she gingerly folded the

dress, dyed with dead men's blood, so that the stiff, dark stains were on the inside, where she wouldn't have to look at them. She stepped back into the circle of light and knelt. She was still shaking, perhaps because the shirt—probably Weiland's—was thinner than her dress had been. More likely it was from all the physical exertion: the running, the extended riding, the constant state of fear. Her heart was beating hard enough to hurt, leaving a metallic taste in her throat. She was too old for this, she reminded herself: She kept thinking like an almost-seventeen-year-old, when her body was more than fifty years old. She was going to kill herself if she wasn't more careful.

Eventually, Shile brought a blanket for her—stiff and scratchy and smelling of horse, but it felt wonderfully warm.

She stole a glance at him while he wasn't looking. He was kind. He could no doubt be invaluable in rescuing Beryl. She more or less trusted him. But she was afraid. As he clasped her shoulder reassuringly, she put her hand over his and squeezed, wishing one of her extra years onto him. It was not as though, she assured herself, it would ever come to make a difference: With the life he and Weiland led, neither was likely to see forty, and one more year off their old age would never be missed.

He gave her his vacant though amiable smile and began poking at the fire.

Weiland came carrying his sheathed sword and crouched next to her, the sword across his knees.

"I want to thank you for all your help," Lylene said, and momentarily rested her hand on his wrist.

But of all people, she shouldn't have tried it with him. He seized her arm and pulled her down closer to him, closer to the fire. "Whatever the hell you just did," he warned, "don't try it again."

She considered proclaiming her innocence, denying that she'd done anything. Instead, she just whispered, "No."

"Weiland," Shile said, confused and earnest. "*Weiland.*"

Slowly he released her arm.

She sat back on her heels, wishing she could move farther away from him without looking like a cringing dog.

Shile sat down, crosslegged, and warmed his hands at the fire. "Now," he said, eager for peace, "tell us what set an obvious lady of quality, such as yourself, into a place like the Happy Wench Inn, desperate enough to seek help from . . . strangers . . . like us."

Lylene was at a loss for words. After her night in the barn, she had picked all the straw she could feel from her hair; but that hair hadn't been combed in two days. Her clothes, before she had changed to men's garb, were filthy. She had been accused—and rightly so—of witchcraft, had engaged in a brawl that had left a half dozen dead, and had run off with two men, strangers, who did this sort of thing for a living. And she was old, more than a half-century old.

Weiland supplied the words she couldn't: "*Obvious* . . . lady of quality?"

Shile didn't take his gaze from her. "Obvious. From the way she carries herself, her walk, her speech, the expression in her eyes: gentrice. Come on hard times, and recently at that." Finally he did look away. "I can understand hard times."

Weiland swore and pulled the long sword from its sheath. Close to her as he was, his arm brushed hers, and this time she shrank back, expecting . . . she wasn't sure what. But he didn't even look at her. To all appearances he had nothing more ominous in mind than to see the weapon properly cleaned after their hasty retreat from Arandell. But she didn't trust the coincidence of the timing nor his apparent lack of attention.

Shile put his hand on her shoulder and said, "Relax. Any time you desire it, you're free to leave."

Hesitantly, Lylene nodded.

"Weiland and I are what you might call free agents . . ."

"Mercenaries." Again her voice wasn't cooperating; it came out a whisper. But she hated the way he danced around words—at least Weiland was honest about what he was.

"Occasionally," Shile admitted. "We do . . . odd jobs. For pay."

"I told you: I have no money."

"Sometimes a situation just gives the impression of being fraught with monetary opportunities."

She had no answer for that.

"This strikes me as just such an occasion. If not, we've wasted a little time, had a little adventure, and tomorrow morning we part amicably, never to see each other again. On the other hand, we may be able to help each other."

Slowly, weighing each word, she nodded.

"So. From the beginning. My name is Shiley—please call me Shile—and this is Weiland."

Weiland looked up from working the edge of the sword and gave a sardonic nod.

"My name is Lylene of Dorstede. My parents were Lord and Lady Delroy."

"Deceased?" Shile asked.

She nodded. "After their deaths, I . . . my sister and I were raised by my aunt. It was her son, Randal, who inherited the Delroy estates. Six months ago Beryl was marrying Randal." It was becoming increasingly difficult to speak.

Shile rested a hand on her arm encouragingly.

"Some men came. Marauders. Lead by a baron named Theron. They took Beryl—forced her to go with them. Nobody was willing to do anything about it: the Church, the neighboring lords . . ."

"What about this cousin," Weiland asked, "this Randal?"

"Dead. He was killed in the raid."

Shile patted her hand gently. "No other cousins? Nobody to redress—"

"Nobody." She gnawed on her lip and tried to compose herself. "The bishop said . . . Theron . . . In the eyes of the Church the two of them are married. After all that: In the eyes of the Church the two of them are married. I'm not telling this well."

"You're doing fine. This sister of yours, she had been widowed before?"

Lylene shook her head. Then saw the problem. "Beryl's only eighteen years old." She saw the looks and knew she strained at their credulity. But she needed to impress on them the urgency of the situation, Beryl's helplessness and innocence. "I'm . . . not as old as I look."

She winced, realizing what she had just said, the counterpart of Harkta's *I'm older than I look*. She covered her face with her hands, speaking between her fingers. "The law seemed to be on Theron's side. And the Church. So I sought the help of a wizard."

She felt Weiland shift uncomfortably.

"He's the one who did this to you?" Shile urged.

She put her hands in her lap and nodded.

Shile glanced at Weiland, who had finally left off with the sword. "You can't trust wizards," Weiland observed dryly.

She hoped he meant that merely as a sympathetic response. If he found out *she* was a wizard, would he recommend abandoning her, or slitting her throat?

Shile ran his hand through his dark hair, then he looked at her levelly. "This wizard. Does he have anything to do with that gold piece that caused such a stir tonight?"

She nodded, slowly. She'd never been a good liar and hoped her face wouldn't give her away, for she certainly wasn't going to trust these two with the truth. "The money was Harkta's. He said that he would help me, but I had to work for him for three months." Could they hear her swallow? "Then, after my time was through . . . he tricked me. He turned me old and threw me out."

She saw Shile and Weiland exchange glances. What were they thinking? "I stole the money." She bit her lip, unable to look either man in the eye, and hoped they'd put her unease down to guilt over the thievery. "It must have been some kind of magic money. But what I paid you with, that was my own. That won't disappear. I swear it won't." Again that look: disbelief? Or chagrin at having misjudged the possibilities of the situation?

Weiland slipped his sword into its sheath and stood, finally giving her space to breathe again.

"Listen." Shile was obviously less willing than his partner to give up. "Why don't we rest for the night? There are possibilities here. We'll talk more tomorrow."

Weiland appeared about to protest. Instead he made a helpless gesture and headed for the horses.

Lylene, hurrying lest Shile change his mind, asked: "You think you can rescue Beryl from Theron?"

"I'm sure of it."

"He lives at Saldemar, and it's highly fortified." She'd heard that often enough from the Dorstede knights. "It's on a hill—"

Shile placed a finger to her lips, silencing her. "We'll rescue her for you. Weiland can get us in. He hired out to Theron a few years back." He raised his voice. "Think Theron will remember you?"

Weiland, checking the horses' tethers, didn't answer.

"We'll rescue her for you," Shile said.

10

Morning was bright and warm. Since they had camped within walking distance of a pond, Lylene decided to bathe.

It was good to be clean, but the goodness was tempered by the sight of her wrinkled skin and her sagging breasts and forearms. True, there had been some improvement. She had wished close to two dozen years onto various people and was no longer bent over with pain. Her hands, though stiff and swollen at the joints, had loosened from the gnarled claws they had been that first day.

Still, she sat in water deep enough to cover to her shoulders so she wouldn't have to see herself, and she cried, softly, hoping that Shile and Weiland wouldn't hear her. And the next moment hoping that they would. She wanted to be held, to be comforted. To be taken care of.

But she remembered she was naked, and she knew what she looked like, and in any case the camp wasn't so close that they could possibly hear her, whether she hoped it or not. And who was there to hold her? Weiland, who was at least as dangerous as Harkta and Theron? Shile, with all his grand plans? She rinsed her face and waded back to the shore to dress in her borrowed clothes.

Tying her grayish-red hair back out of her way, she was scrubbing the blood stains from her dress when from behind a nearby bush she caught the glint of sun on metal. Two thoughts followed, one on top of the other: that despite any other moral deficiencies, neither Shile nor Weiland seemed the kind to skulk behind bushes peeking at bathing women—especially bathing fifty-year-old women—and that the only armor either man wore was padded leather.

Someone from Arandell, most likely: brother or father or son or friend to someone they had killed last night.

Her hands shook, and she dunked the dress into the water to hide them. She paid attention to the sounds around her: the self-satisfied coo of a dove, the buzz of insects. She thought she heard the creak of metal, an armored man shifting weight. As far as she could tell, there was only the one. There had to be others, but where? Had they found the camp already? Not likely, or this one wouldn't be quietly watching her, waiting for her to lead him to her companions. On the other hand, given enough time, this one's friends would find the camp anyway, and overrun it without warning. Given enough time . . . She had already been gone too long. How much time before Shile or Weiland came looking for her and walked into a trap?

She swished the dress around in the water, grazing her knuckles on a submerged stone. If she returned to the camp, that would give the two young mercenaries at least a few moments' warning. She forced herself to regulate her breathing, sure that her watcher must be growing suspicious by now. She would be between them: between the pursuers from Arandell and their prey.

And there was nothing else she could do.

Once more her hand brushed the underwater stone. It was sharp and slightly bigger than her clenched fist. With no plan in mind, but because a rock seemed a good thing to have at a time like this, she tucked it into a fold of her dress. Sure that she must be acting unnaturally enough to alert even a simpleton, she wrung the dress, never looking in the direction of the bush. With the sodden dress wadded in her arms, she started back the way she had come.

Her back prickled, from sweat, from the knowledge that behind her was someone who wanted to see her dead. She kept walking, her eyes forward.

There was a crunch of underbrush from behind but to the side: Someone—or possibly more than one—had joined the first stalker. The whistle of a warbler sounded from off to her right. She realized she had heard an inordinate number of warblers this morning. That was the fourth or fifth since she left the pond. If each call represented one man, plus the one who had been watching all along, plus the two (she was sure of it now) who had joined . . . And there were horses out there amongst the trees, too: She heard the muffled jangle as one shook its reins.

She recognized the lightning-struck spruce. From this angle of approach, the camp wasn't that obvious until one was practically in it.

Surely the men who followed must smell the smoke from the camp cookfire.

She gauged the distance, how long it would take to traverse it at a run, and screamed, "Shile! Weiland! Ambush!"

Behind her, the woods erupted into sound: men and horses crashing through, no longer intent on secrecy. She stumbled over a root, half-falling into the clearing. Shile was standing, facing her direction, his sword drawn. Weiland was moving in to his side, holding an oversized bow with an arrow already nocked.

Lylene saw her mistake at once: She had led the men of Arandell in at an angle to keep them from seeing the camp until the last moment, but this had brought them in between the campfire and the horses. There would be no chance for flight.

Weiland's arrow whizzed over her head, close enough that she thought he had aimed at her, suspecting betrayal. But from behind she heard a cry and a thud, and a riderless horse crashed through the thicket, narrowly missing her.

Her outstretched hand kept her from falling. Now, as she started to straighten, Weiland called, "Down!" and he loosed another arrow that cut the air just above her head.

She began running in a low crouch, still holding on to her dripping dress, following the perimeter of the clearing to get herself out of the fighters' way.

"My Lady!" Shile was on the move, trying to get to her while Weiland covered them. She headed for him, out of Weiland's range now and able to run upright.

A horseman broke into the clearing, then a second. One of Weiland's arrows hit the first, but by then there were three more. He fit another arrow to the bow but took a step back before releasing.

Shile grabbed Lylene's free arm and yelled

Weiland's name. Weiland began to retreat, slowly, toward the trees on the far side of the clearing. Shile directed Lylene in a path designed to intercept him. More and more men poured into the clearing, men on foot as well as those who were mounted, spreading out to cut off escape into the woods.

Shile released her arm, and Lylene saw that three of the horsemen were headed directly at them.

The one in the forefront had developed too great a lead. Shile sidestepped the swing of his sword, then brought his own weapon up into the man's abdomen, and there was no one close enough to take Shile at disadvantage.

But the remaining two came at them together.

Closer.

Closer.

She braced herself.

One toppled from his horse, one of Weiland's arrows in his back, and by then the remaining horseman was level with Shile.

He swung his sword at Shile's head. Shile took the force of the blow on his own upraised sword. He wasn't nearly as good at this as Weiland.

Lylene watched in fascinated horror, twisting the wet dress she still held. Weiland was running toward them, but there was no way he could reach Shile in time. She took a step forward as Shile's opponent raised his blade again. Foolishness. What could she do to help, an old woman brandishing a wet dress? What good would getting killed serve? But they were in this because of her, and she wasn't going to abandon them. She had abandoned Beryl, and she wasn't ever going to abandon anybody again.

She swung her dress at the man. There was an audible *clunk!* as the forgotten river rock put a dent in his helmet. The man dropped.

Lylene was torn between hoping she had killed him and fearing that she hadn't.

"Some dress," Weiland acknowledged, running past as she lingered in guilty numbness. She glimpsed the remaining horsemen, seeing the surprise on their faces before Shile spun her around. They were just fumbling with their bows as she and Shile broke through the edge of the clearing, close on Weiland's heels.

11

They burst into the woods, weaving, always looking for ways that would tax the pursuing horses yet be clear enough that they themselves could pass rapidly. But they still heard their pursuers behind them. And then to the left. And finally outflanking them to the right.

"This way." Shile pulled her toward a rocky hill.

They scrambled up, and she bent over, resting her hands on her knees, afraid she was going to retch from the exertion. And from the realization of how many men had died back there—and that she might have killed one of them. Still, she managed to look around. Too open. She didn't have enough breath to give voice to the words.

But surely they could see as well as she.

There just wasn't any place better.

Weiland peered into the distance, examining the landscape or checking for pursuers—Lylene couldn't tell.

Out of breath himself, though he was half Lylene's age, Shile asked, "What do you think?"

Weiland shook his head.

"Any more-helpful thoughts?"

Weiland paused, catching his breath also. "If one of us headed off down the south slope, back into the woods, that might draw them off, or at least divide them."

"Divide us, too."

"There is that to consider," Weiland admitted.

Several men appeared, coming through the trees. Then more, in from both sides. They drew their horses in to confer. Thirteen in all.

"Can we defend the hill?" Shile asked.

Weiland held up his nearly empty quiver.

"Let's see. At thirteen of them, three of us, and five arrows . . . Think you can hit two and a half of them with each shot?"

"Probably not."

"Probably not," Shile agreed. "You stay here with Lady Lylene and the bow. I'll try to draw them off."

"Or the other way?"

Shile indicated Weiland's bow. "I could never use that thing. Even if you'd brought your short bow, I'd be more likely to hit my own foot than any of them. You can do more good here."

"You'll only get lost in the forest, and we'll have to come looking for you."

"Toss a coin for it?"

"Not with you."

"You know I'm right." Shile grinned at Weiland, then took Lylene's sweaty hand and raised it to his lips.

Lylene, who had thought she'd caught her breath, found she couldn't breathe again. "Wait." She looked from one to the other. "I don't understand what's happening."

Shile kissed her hand. "Stay with Weiland. We'll regroup when we can."

Lylene grabbed his arm. "They'll leave a few men here to guard us, then the rest will go after you and tear you apart like a pack of hungry dogs. And then they'll come back and get us."

"Lady Lylene." Shile pulled free of her. His dark eyes were disturbed. He had obviously meant to do this quickly. As though her fear were catching, his face began to show the strain despite his best intentions.

From below, someone barked an order: The men separated to spread out around the hill. Shile firmly handed her over to Weiland, who told her: "You handled yourself well down there. Don't lose control now."

"You'll have the bow," Shile added. "They don't know we're almost out of arrows."

"*They* have bows, too," Lylene protested.

"They have crossbows," Weiland said.

"So?"

"This is a long bow." That meant nothing to her. It just looked terribly ungainly, giving Weiland the appearance, despite his height, of a child playing with an adult's weapon. "A Welsh bow." That didn't help either. "It has more range."

"More range than a crossbow?" Lylene asked incredulously.

"Yes," Shile and Weiland told her together. Shile made to leave again, and Lylene, again, grabbed his arm.

This time Weiland swore at her and took her by the shoulders, but she demanded: "So if you had more arrows, you could shoot at them while they couldn't shoot at us?"

"*If* we had more arrows," Weiland said. "Lady, there's at least a chance this way. Let him go or you'll be the sure death of him."

"I can make more arrows," Lylene said.

"So could either of us," Weiland snapped.

"I can make more arrows in the time it'll take those men to get into range for their crossbows."

That got their attention.

"My Lady?" said Shile.

Weiland's hand dropped from her shoulder.

Ignoring Shile's skeptical look, she took the five arrows and set them on the ground before her. Gently she rested her hands on them. She closed her eyes and concentrated. One of the men, Weiland or Shile, inhaled sharply. She spread the ten arrows out and concentrated again. Spread the twenty arrows out and concentrated again. Spread the forty and concentrated again.

"Mother of God," Shile whispered.

Lylene gathered up a handful of the arrows and held them out. "I can make more," she offered. More deaths which would be her doing. But the alternative was dying.

Shile looked ready to hug her. He grinned, took the handful, and turned to hand them to Weiland.

But Weiland took a step back, away from the hand that held the arrows, all the while staring at Lylene.

"Weiland," Shile said. "*Weiland.*"

Lylene had to turn from the look on his face. There was a certain element of fear, of horror, but mostly what she read was betrayal.

"Weiland," Shile urged between clenched teeth. "We're almost in their range."

Weiland backed another step from her.

Shile snatched the bow from him, nocked an arrow, and released it into the advancing line. It curved low, hitting the ground near the feet of one of the horses. The horse skittered. The rider maintained control. Shile released another arrow. It came close to hitting one of the men but, mostly spent, bounced harmlessly off his mail sleeve. The men of Arandell were becoming skittish. They could see that the weapon Shile held could outdistance theirs, despite his lack of skill. They were obviously trying to decide whether to retreat or to rush the remaining distance so they could bring their own weapons into play.

"Weiland," Shile said, "you're going to get all of us killed."

Weiland glanced at him, the first he had looked away from Lylene.

Shile shook the bow at him.

Reluctantly, Weiland took it.

"Take the arrows. *Weiland.*"

Looking like a man who is knowingly condemning his soul to hell, Weiland took the arrows. He drew on the bow, and even Lylene, unfamiliar with weaponry, saw that he pulled with much more strength and decisiveness than Shile. The arrow whistled through the air and hit the chest of the man who had been shouting the orders. In the time it took the arrow to make the flight, Weiland had readied and fired another.

At the third arrow, they started to back off. At the fifth, they turned and ran. They stopped under the branches of the surrounding trees, well out of any bow's range, and drew together to confer.

By then, Weiland had shot eight arrows,

with only the last a clean miss. Five men lay motionless, another had been hit in the thigh and was laboriously crawling toward his fellows at the fringe of the forest, and one more had kept on his horse and was being seen to. Weiland fit another arrow to the string, sighting on the crawling man. But perhaps he took pity. Or, at the last, he decided the man had gotten beyond his range, for he lowered the bow unfired.

Lylene stared at the body-littered ground. It was too much like the wedding feast. She prayed for all the wasted life, and she prayed for the survivors, and—since Father Tobias had taught her it was presumptuous to dictate one's desires to God—she prayed that His will be done, with the fervent hope that His will was that she and Shile and Weiland would remain among the survivors.

Shile paused to give her shoulder a reassuring squeeze, then he went to join Weiland, who had crouched down and was watching the remnant of their attackers as though, with enough concentration, he could discern their plans from here. Shile stooped down next to him. Lylene watched them with their heads together—Shile's dark and curly hair almost touching Weiland's long and pale. They spoke too quietly for her to make out the words. But a look, a set of the back and shoulders, a tone deciphered without benefit of the actual words: Lylene had just realized the men were arguing when Shile glanced back at her and motioned for her to join them.

Hesitantly she approached, crouching also.

Weiland took the excuse of keeping watch on the remaining soldiers and didn't face her.

He was afraid of her, of her magic. She had been drawn to him, and simultaneously repelled by him, and all the while—the clearest feeling—frightened of him. And here he was, afraid of her.

She liked him better for it: this proof that he was human after all. And she liked herself less, that she should feel that way.

"We owe our lives to you," Shile told her.

"And I to you. Several times over."

"If," Shile said, "we are to make full use of this gift you have given us, we must understand it fully. My Lady Lylene, now is not the time for secrets."

Lylene followed Weiland's lead and scrutinized the men at the forest's edge. Leaderless, they appeared unable to settle on a course of action. Various ones would glance in their direction, or point at them, or beyond them, or back toward Arandell, and so far made no decisive move.

"My Lady,"—Shile shifted his weight—"are you a witch?"

"No," she said. "I mean, I don't think so. That is, not really."

Weiland, his face pale and strained, shot her a wary glance.

"I'm not trying to be evasive. It's just I'm new to all this."

"New?" Shile jumped on the word. "You weren't born to this power?" She shook her head, and he made the connection. "This wizard of yours . . ."

"Harkta. Yes. My bargain with Harkta was that he teach me magic. I thought it could help me rescue my sister. But my only power is to duplicate things. That seemed little enough. Last night was the first I learned that what I make doesn't even last."

"*Things?*" Shile repeated. "What? Coins, arrows . . . ?"

"Clothes." She shrugged apologetically, for not being more knowledgeable, more helpful.

Shile waited for her to go on.

"Whatever I touch, I suppose."

Weiland interrupted. "Is now the time—"

"Horses?" Shile asked. "Could you do horses?"

"They'd need to be here, first," she reminded him.

He grabbed her by the shoulders so that she fell back, sitting on her heels. "But you *could* do them, living creatures?"

"I suppose. I never tried."

"And only the duplicate disappears, not the original?"

"Yes, but—"

"And the duplicate doesn't disappear for at least several hours?"

"Yes, but—"

"And it's just like the original, no one can tell the difference?"

"Yes, but—"

"Jesus," Weiland whispered.

Lylene still had her mind so set on horses that she assumed Weiland had seen something in the gathering below. But a glance assured her that the situation hadn't changed, and Weiland wasn't looking there anyway, but—with his face even whiter than before—at Shile. She glanced from Weiland to Shile and felt the color drain from her own face as she realized what Weiland had guessed, what Shile must mean. "You?" She whispered also. "Make a duplicate of you?"

"Can you?"

"Surely you're not serious."

"Why not? There's seven of them, two of us—that trick with the dress was neatly done, my Lady, but you'll not get away with it more than the once. They're not going to try a frontal assault again. They'll circle around and pick us off from the back, where they'll have more cover, or—if they're in no hurry and want to play it safe—they'll dig in and starve us out."

"Shile," Weiland said. *"Shile."*

"And the fact that the duplicates don't last is all for the best," Shile said. "How would we ever feed all those extra mouths?"

Weiland put his back to them, refusing this madness. But then he whipped around again. "Shile, be sensible—"

Shile reached into a pocket at his belt and pulled out a coin. "Toss you for it?" he volunteered, and sent the coin spinning through the air, then caught it against his arm.

Weiland grabbed his wrist. "Would you—"

"I have no idea what will happen to you," Lylene interrupted, "when I make the magic, or when the . . . second you . . . goes . . . wherever it goes."

Weiland jerked back around to face the men of Arandell.

Shile took her hand. She felt a tremor in his hand, but he covered it by bringing her fingers to his lips. "It's our only chance."

"Shile—"

"You need to stop worrying about everything that could go wrong. You need to learn to make your wager, hope for the best, and just go ahead and throw the dice."

This from someone who no doubt knew how to cheat at dice.

He squeezed her hand. "Standing? Kneeling? What's the best way?"

"I don't know." She placed a hand on his head. The dark hair was fine and surprisingly soft. He twitched a nervous smile as she wondered what to do next. Unbidden came the memory of one of the young scullery maids at home telling in delighted horror how a witch would consecrate herself to Satan: Crouching on her toes, one hand on top of her head, the other under her heels, three times the would-be witch repeated, *All that I hold between my hands, I offer now to you.* Lylene shifted her hand to Shile's shoulder, putting her other hand on the opposite shoulder. "I don't know if this will hurt," she said. She almost refused then, faced with that look of trusting apprehension.

Weiland was steadfastly not watching them, resting his head against his knee.

She closed her eyes. She pictured Shile as he had been at the Happy Wench Inn—when he caught her eye across the hostile crowd and motioned for her to join him. She thought of his dark, always bemused eyes, of the soft hair she had just touched. He was in danger because of her. Forced to leave Arandell because of her. Pursued because of her. Risking his life, perhaps his very soul—

She thought he had twisted, balking at the last moment. A heartbeat's worth of relief. But her arms were extended, the left still going forward to rest gently on one shoulder, the right stretched wide and resting—God help her—on another shoulder. She opened her eyes and snatched back her hands with a stifled cry. Two Shiles looked back at her. The only difference was that the one on her right gave a jaunty smile, while the left one looked about to be sick.

"It didn't hurt," the right-hand Shile said, taking her hand, smiling. "Everything is fine."

The left-hand Shile snatched her hand away, forced her to pay attention to him. "Again," he said.

She shook her head, trembling. "I can't."

"You can. You did with the arrows. It doesn't hurt. I didn't feel anything." He glanced up at Weiland. "Are we getting any reaction?"

Weiland, who she wouldn't have thought could get any paler, seemed to be having trouble breathing.

"Hey!" Shile shouted. "Are you jackals paying attention?"

Lylene saw that, indeed, several of the people gathered at the forest edge were pointing and talking excitedly.

"Again," Shile said.

She put her hands around both Shiles. This time her right hand slipped away, unable to contain the four men who crouched before her.

"Again," two of them said simultaneously.

"Enough." Weiland gazed at them with an expression that was hard to look at, that no doubt mirrored her own, and had Shile any sense, she should have found the same on his face. "*Enough,* Shile."

"They're going," Lylene said, seeing that the makeshift army from Arandell suddenly couldn't get under cover of the forest fast enough. "They don't want anything to do with us. Please, Shile, no more." She covered her face with her hands because she couldn't be sure which of the four she should be addressing. She felt him—one of him—get up. Someone patted her shoulder. Someone else said, "My Lady, everything's fine. Don't be upset."

She jumped, found two Shiles kneeling before her, another hovering anxiously nearby, and one standing next to Weiland—watching the scrambled retreat.

The one with his hand on her shoulder smiled, Shile's quirky smile exactly. The other who knelt leaned forward to caress her hair from her face, and gave the same smile.

She cringed away from both of them.

"My Lady . . ." said the one who was standing—not the same who had spoken before: It was the same voice but from a different location.

"Weiland," she begged, but Weiland, still in

a low crouch, was staring up at the Shile who stood next to him.

That Shile rested a hand on his shoulder. "It's all right," he said. He smiled at Lylene to include her. "Really. Everything is fine."

Lylene put her hands over her ears. "Shile!" she screamed. She could only complicate matters by getting hysterical, but she was unable to stem the growing waves of panic. "I can't tell the difference! Shile!"

The one who had been standing near her approached. "My Lady, it's me," and all the others nodded agreement. The two who had been kneeling realized the effect they were having on her; and, true to Shile's solicitious nature, they backed off, giving her breathing room.

The real Shile, the first one, knelt before her. He took her hand and squeezed, trying to reassure her with the same anxious smile she had seen on three other faces only moments past.

"They're all gone," said the one who was watching their attackers. "Perhaps we should move quickly—before they talk themselves into believing that they mis-saw and get their courage back." He had distanced himself from Weiland, probably for the identical reason the others had done the same for her. Mindful of Weiland's pride, he stalked the edge of the hill as though merely searching for the best vantage.

Her Shile stood, and Lylene, still clutching his hand, scrambled to her feet also. He went to Weiland, who watched his approach warily. Lylene forced herself to let go of his hand. One of the others smiled shyly, and she did her best to smile back.

Another picked up the quiver and started filling it with the arrows that lay scattered where Weiland had dropped them. Finished, he approached hesitantly. "These are the made ones," he said, handing Weiland the quiver, "and these are the originals."

"Better keep them separate," a second said.

The third nodded. "The made ones will be gone by dusk."

Weiland took both batches of arrows without a word and finally remembered to close his mouth, finally remembered to breathe.

"We better get back to the horses." The original Shile took hold of Weiland's arm and pulled him to his feet.

"If they're still there." All four Shiles said this last part, like a chorus of monks joining in for an antiphon.

Weiland stole a glance at her—he knew who was responsible for this state of affairs—and started down the hill.

"Somebody—" the original Shile started, but the others anticipated him: One was already moving to take the lead, another went down the back way, apparently to scout out possible ambush, and the last fell in behind, to guard their backs.

Shile took a steadying breath, then held out his hand to help Lylene.

Lylene tried very hard not to think of anything.

12

They found their horses much as they had left them, the chestnut munching at a clump of grass, looking disconsolate at having been ignored so long, the bay stamping restively. The third Shile, who had circled round to check for ambush or stragglers, hadn't caught up yet.

Weiland went to see to his horse, which nipped at him to show that all was not so readily forgiven, but allowed itself to be scratched between the eyes nonetheless. Lylene clung to her Shile's arm as one of the other Shiles fussed over the chestnut, and the second other Shile moved among the dead bodies, occasionally turning one over with his foot for a closer look.

"He's not stealing from the dead, is he?" Lylene asked.

Shile, also watching his double, said, "I don't know."

"No." The one who was tending the horse appeared shocked at her question, and even more so that Shile didn't know the answer. "Of course not."

Shile shook his head as though to clear it. He seemed to remember he was, to all purposes, talking about himself. "No," he said. "Checking for survivors."

The man had stooped down beside one of the bodies and stayed there. Now he looked in their direction, and Shile pulled loose of Lylene's grasp. "I won't be long."

Lylene watched his retreating back. That way she didn't have to look at any of the strangers who bore his face, nor at Weiland.

The Shile nearest her cleared his throat. "We're . . . ahm, going to need more horses."

"Not with my horse you don't," Weiland growled.

"Actually, it'd be better with Whitcomb." The man scratched under the chestnut's cheek. "Wouldn't it, boy? You're more used to us."

And indeed, if the horse was disconcerted about seeing three Shiles, it gave no indication. Lylene couldn't help but consider it a betrayal.

Weiland looked from horse to man, opened his mouth, closed it again, shot her a look of pure loathing, and turned his back on all of them.

"Put the saddle on first," Lylene advised. Same face, that was obvious, same voice, same mannerisms. They must smell the same, feel the same, that the horse couldn't tell the difference. Her head was beginning to hurt. They must think the same, share the memories—for that one had known the horse's name. She glanced at the two Shiles crouched together talking, and she could not tell which was which. The sun glinted off metal—weapon or armor of one of the fallen men. She blinked against the brightness and was left with an afterimage of dark trees looming above her. She brushed her hair from her face and realized her face was hot, her hand was shaking. As from a great distance, she watched Weiland stamp out the campfire, which was almost burned out anyway, breakfast an unrecognizable cinder. Inexplicably, her heart was racing and she was filled with a definite though nameless dread. It was suddenly hard for her to breathe, to swallow. She saw a fleeting image of an overgrown gully, a stream she didn't recognize. A hand touched her arm, and she jumped with a gasp.

That Shile took a step back from her, his hands held out to show no harm was intended. "I'm sorry. I didn't mean to startle you. You look unwell. Do you want me to call Shile?" He must mean the real one.

"No, I just . . . This place . . ." She glanced around, unable to shake the feeling that she had been running, that she was being closed in upon. Her nostrils were filled with the scents of sweat and forest.

She put her hands on Shile's horse and concentrated. Weiland's bay reared, whinnying at the appearance of a new horse. The two chestnuts shied away from each other.

Weiland grabbed hold of his horse's reins, tried to calm it.

"My Lady," the Shile who wasn't Shile said to her, "are you sure you're—"

She put a shaking hand on the forehead of each of the chestnut horses and, ignoring the unreasonable fear which had beset her, concentrated again.

The nearby Shile jerked on her arm, and she fell against him, out of range of the four chestnuts, one of whose skittish hooves had come close to striking her.

Sun glinted on metal, again stabbing at her eyes. "Get away!" She shoved at him, and he took a step back. "Shile." Her voice was little more than a whisper. "Shile!"

But the original Shile was too far away to hear.

"Shile!" The duplicate who stood near her raised his voice, and—from very, very far away—Shile looked up.

And the sword she felt suspended above her plunged.

She screamed, falling backward, though she

had the sensation that she was already with her back to the mossy ground of the stream bank—down and with nowhere to go. Her body was afire with pain and twitched convulsively. The scream echoed in her skull, worse pain yet. Fighting, trying to hold on with fingernails and willpower, she felt life slipping away, running out onto the ground like so much spilled water.

Someone was cradling her head, was holding her down to prevent her from doing injury to herself, and was gently rocking her, repeating calm, meaningless reassurances as one might do for a sick child or injured animal.

She opened her eyes, saw that it was Weiland, of all people. A final shudder worked its way through her body, and he held her tighter apparently afraid another fit was starting.

"What happened? My God . . ." One of the Shiles threw himself to his knees beside her, took her hand and started rubbing it. Two of the others stood nearby, looking afraid that they might be the cause of her distress. *The* two others, she corrected herself.

"He's dead."

Weiland and the Shile who held her hand both leaned closer to hear her whisper.

"What?" Shile asked.

"Who?" Weiland asked.

"Shile. The . . . other Shile." She swallowed, her throat raw. "I felt him die."

Shile caressed the hair away from her face.

"Did you," Weiland asked, "*feel* . . . any details?" All three Shiles gave him the same hard look, which he shrugged off. "Was it our pursuers? All of them?"

"I don't know. I think so. I couldn't see that clearly. He was panicked, chased. They were closing in. I saw a sword." She turned her face away from them, felt Weiland rest his hand on her head.

"Any survivors here?" Shile's voice. From one of the ones who wasn't really Shile, to the one who had been checking the bodies.

"No," that one said.

"You took a long time," Lylene said, "for no survivors."

"There was one, my Lady, but he was badly wounded."

"He would have died anyway," Shile added.

"I understand," she said. And she did. But it was a reminder of just what these friends of hers were.

"We should get moving." Shile got to his feet. "My Lady, are you well enough to travel?"

She glanced back at Weiland, suddenly self-conscious about being in his lap. Just as he looked chagrined with himself for having been caught at gentleness. One of the Shiles helped her stand. Weiland pointedly ignored the hand offered him.

Shile swung up onto one of the chestnut horses, unconcerned—or not showing his concern—about which was the original. "It'd probably be safest to avoid the Arandell road, head off to the southeast, then circle round Cragsfall to Saldemar."

The duplicate who had helped her stand now helped her get up behind Shile.

One of the others untethered the bay horse, and Weiland snatched the reins from him, then mounted, looking sullen and stubborn.

The man didn't take offense. He went through his own saddlebag and pulled out a red handkerchief, which he tied at his throat. "Maybe this will help lessen the confusion," he said equably. "You can call me Duncan."

The other, already mounted, had found a strip of leather that he tied around his head, to hold back his hair and make him distinct from the others. "I'll be Jerel."

"We'll say that it was Newlin who died." Duncan looked vaguely toward Arandell. "No one should die without a name."

Weiland went pale again, looked from Shile to Shile to Shile, swore, and headed out of the clearing.

Under the clatter of leaving, Lylene asked Shile, "What's wrong with those particular names?"

"Just that they're ones I've used previously."

She thought he sounded more shaken than he would have her know.

"What about Newlin? Shouldn't we try to find—" She remembered and rested her head on Shile's back, dizzy and nauseated. He patted her hand, and neither gave voice to the obvious: Come the next day, burial would make no difference.

13

The large destriers were more than Lylene could manage by herself, so she rode with someone, shifting periodically so as not to over tax any one animal. Now that Duncan and Jerel had names, as well as a means to tell them apart, they were less intimidating. Lylene still found their tendency to finish each other's sentences disconcerting.

At one point while she was riding with Duncan, and he and Jerel were telling her a long, convoluted story about a larcenous monk, Weiland—looking particularly sour—shouldered his horse past them.

Duncan and Jerel took up their story again as though they hadn't noticed. But Lylene, casting an annoyed look at Weiland's back, saw him pull alongside of Shile, and, with the slightest inclination of his head, indicate his empty quiver.

Lylene looked at Jerel, suddenly unable to

make sense of his words. Unlikely that he had caught Weiland's gesture, or seen that the arrows she had made had faded away, though it was hard to be certain. She found herself getting angry at the two of them, Duncan and Jerel. Couldn't they understand the seriousness of their situation? How could they remain so unremittingly cheerful? But that wasn't fair. They understood their situation at least as well as she.

Maybe, she thought, maybe the amount of energy she put into making her duplicates counted for something. The things she had created before—cloaks and money and arrows—had meant nothing to her. She had created them almost off-handedly, while with Shile she had been thinking how very fond she was of him. She had been shaking with the emotion of the moment, concentrating so hard her body had ached, and afterward . . . afterward she had felt drained. Surely that counted for something? Would wishing give these duplicates life beyond the short span she had given the arrows that she had known were for immediate use?

Jerel and Duncan's voices had died away. Whether they had finished their story, she had no idea. Shile, from up ahead, announced that they were coming on a village and that they would stop there to eat and rest the horses, and never a mention that they had already had a long stop just a little while back.

Jerel patted her hand, as Shile was wont to do.

The people of the village gathered about them, silent and apprehensive. A moment before, everything had been noisy activity: men and women working in the surrounding fields, or churning butter, or gathering kindling sticks, or—in the case of one young couple—bickering bitterly while rethatching the roof of a cottage. Now the silence was broken only by a baby crying and by one youngster, squealing and clattering his milk pail, who chased after a runaway goat that zigzagged amongst the cottages.

The headman of the village approached, wiping his hands on his tunic.

"I'll handle this," Shile whispered, obviously feeling that the uncanny resemblance among the three of them would be cause enough for unease without Duncan and Jerel complicating things by opening their mouths.

"Welcome," the headman said, sounding as though he meant the opposite. "My Lords. M'Lady." There was no way he could have taken them for members of the nobility. No doubt he hoped his addressing them as such would be flattering and that, flattered, they might leave him and his people alone.

Shile nodded. "My companions and I have been traveling all day, and we have need of food and rest."

The man started to point off to the right, but before he could get a word out, Shile said: "We shall stay here."

The man gave a slight bow. "As you please, my Lord. But as you can see, Tiswold is but a small village, and we have no inn nor any accommodations such as my Lords and Lady—"

"We have traveled far and hard, and one of your cottages turned over to our use until tomorrow morning will suit perfectly."

Again the bow, though if he believed their bedraggled appearance was due to a hard ride, he'd believe anything.

"We will pay for any slight inconvenience we may cause."

The man bowed yet again, looking better pleased about it this time. "One cottage will suffice for my Lords and Lady?"

Shile grinned. "We're all family."

The man's eyes darted nervously amongst them, then he bowed again.

He escorted them to the doorway of one of the larger dwellings, where he introduced himself as Fitch, the village headman, and the owner of the cottage. He invited them to take their evening meal outside, saying it was the villagers' custom, weather permitting.

Long tables were set up, and they sat with Fitch and several others, though each household had its own food. Theirs was a thin, though tasty, vegetable stew.

Shile sat on Lylene's left, and Weiland next to him. Several times the people on that end of the table tried to strike up a conversation, but Weiland would give one-word answers, or none at all, or look at them as though they were fools for whatever they had just said, and eventually they gave up.

On her right, Jerel and Duncan did better. They joked and chatted with their neighbors, seeming totally at ease. Nobody asked them who they were or why they were there. Nobody commented when Duncan referred to Shile and Jerel as his brothers, and moments later Jerel—not having heard—called them his cousins. The conversation paused . . . then resumed.

The air had already gotten chilly before the end of the meal, but Lylene couldn't bring herself to return to the close quarters of their borrowed cottage. Her head had begun to ache and she felt desperate for fresh air. But the villagers quickly stripped the tables and returned them indoors, then disappeared themselves.

In the fading light she strolled along the edge of the cultivated fields. From behind, there was a step, the crack of a twig—scant warning before someone had hold of her. She jerked around, breaking the man's grip, ready to scream and struggle, before she recognized Shile holding out a blanket for her, protection from the evening's damp.

"Sorry," he said. "I seem determined to startle you." He put the blanket around her. "The cottage may not be much, but at least it's warmer than out here." He didn't move but stood looking into her eyes, smiling as though he could see more than the fifty-year-old woman she appeared. She wasn't used to thinking of herself as pretty—even when she'd been her true age, no one had ever called her pretty except the innkeeper at Branford, and she certainly didn't count that. But standing here, looking into Shile's eyes by starlight, exasperating as he could be, she wondered if he found her pretty.

He gave his gentle, quirky smile and brushed a loose strand of her hair out from the blanket. He hesitated a moment, then said: "Better come, before Shile starts worrying about you."

And that was the first she noticed the scarf, all but indistinguishable in the dark: Duncan, and not Shile after all.

She turned, the ache in her head suddenly remembered—and the wrinkles, and the sagging flesh.

Perhaps he didn't notice, for he hooked his arm around hers and headed back toward the cottage.

"Duncan . . ." she started.

But he was looking upward, at the bright stars clear in the crisp air. "I heard somewhere that each falling star represents someone's soul being called to heaven." Duncan stopped walking and gave the sky all his attention. "When I—" he started, then amended it to: "When Shile was very young, he had a dog once . . . which died. Shile's mother told him that even though most animals don't have souls, God makes a special dispensation for pets and allows them into heaven." He suddenly turned on her. "Do you think that's true?"

"I . . . don't know." She didn't know what to make of this mood either, which didn't seem characteristic of Shile. Before she could add to her lame answer, he suddenly started pulling her along again, so fast that she tripped and would have fallen twice except that he held her up. The jostling made her already aching head throb.

"We're late," he told her.

"For what?"

"For Shile wanting to see you."

She was too breathless from their pace to question him. But despite all that, he abandoned her a few feet from the cottage. "Jerel's waiting for me in the barn," he told her, practically pushing her toward the door.

At the doorway she turned back to see him

running between two smaller cottages on the way to where the horses were being kept. Shaking her head, she opened the door.

Shile was sitting at the table, surrounded by feathers and newly made arrowshafts. He glanced up and smiled but quickly returned his attention to his fletching.

She moved the candle by whose light he was working, saying, "You're going to set your hair on fire, if you don't watch out." When he still didn't say anything, she added, "Duncan seemed to think you wanted to see me."

Again the smile. "I always like to see you."

Thank goodness the light was bad enough that he probably couldn't see her blush. "Yes, but he seemed anxious to have me in here—"

Inside her head, something shattered. She probably screamed, though she wasn't sure. She felt that she was falling, although the sensation lasted far longer than it would have taken for her to reach the floor, so she couldn't be sure of that either. What she was sure of was that there had been a glass vessel in her head and that it had suddenly burst. It sent jagged shards up through her brain and out her skull, taking with them the lives of Duncan, with his concerns about God and souls, and Jerel, whose concerns she had never learned. She put her hands to her head, trying to hold the sharp pieces in, willing to endure the pain, if that would save the men she had brought into the world. She screamed their names, begging them to come back, offering to go with them in repentance for what she had done, but already reality was rebuilding itself around her—she felt Shile's arms around her, heard him calling her name—and she knew they had gone, like Newlin, leaving her behind.

She opened her eyes. Shile was bent over her, his face gray and damp with sweat.

The door flung open and Weiland burst in, his sword drawn. His eyes went from Lylene and Shile on the floor, around the room, back to Lylene. "Jesus," he whispered.

She began to shake, and didn't stop for a long time.

14

For all the clarity of the evening sky, the next day dawned gray and damp. They broke their fast on the cold remains of stew, hoping to be out of the village of Tiswold as quickly as possible and to cause as little stir as possible. No one had come to investigate Lylene's screams last night, and no one came this morning. What the villagers presumed or feared was anybody's guess.

Lylene sat huddled in one of the blankets while Shile and Weiland gathered together their few belongings. After an endless night of staring at the underside of the cottage's thatching, Lylene suddenly found herself hard pressed to keep her eyes open.

Shile knelt before her, taking her hand, providing warmth at last. "My Lady, we have brought enough attention on ourselves. We should be leaving." She started to rise, but he didn't move, didn't let go of her hand. "My Lady, I hate to ask this of you. . . . I did promise that we would pay for our lodgings, and our funds are rather limited. . . ."

"It won't last," she said, as though he—of all people—needed reminding. "Shile, the money's no good."

"Of course it's good."

"It won't last."

With an oath, Weiland rammed his sword into its sheath and left, slamming the door.

How slow could they be? "Don't you see, anybody that you paid today . . . Oh." How slow could *she* be? "They would have let us stay without," she said.

"I know. But the promise assured us a more favorable welcome."

"It's like stealing." Lylene felt light-headed, as though she were on the brink of falling asleep. Or of awakening. That was a thought. Would she find in another moment that Shile's duplicates were still here, waiting to be lost all over again? Or perhaps that the whole past day had been a dream and they had never existed at all? Cold comfort, that: The ache was just as real.

She jerked upright. She'd closed her eyes and couldn't be sure how much time had passed. Shile still knelt, one hand holding hers, the other a handful of small coins. She had had no dream: Duncan and Jerel were dead.

She took the coins. It needed less energy to

duplicate them than it would take to stand afterward. She held the two batches out to Shile. "The one on the left is always the original." But he knew that, too, from personal experience.

"My Lady," he murmured.

The villagers were waiting outside. Some of them made pretense of being busy with their day to day activities, but they were all waiting. Weiland brought the horses, two of them: one bay and one chestnut. The villagers stayed clear of him.

Fitch, the headman, swallowed visibly when he saw her, then forced himself to approach Shile. "If my Lords—"

"We're not lords," Shile corrected wearily.

"If you'll be requiring anything else to set you on your journey—"

"Nothing." Shile held out some coins. "We thank you for your hospitality."

Fitch stared at the money, swallowed again. He looked at the three of them, then, apprehensively, behind them, at the closed door of the cottage. "Your two . . ."—he obviously weighed Duncan's "brothers" against Jerel's "cousins"— ". . . kinsmen . . ."

"Gone." Shile kept his voice even. "They left ahead of us, during the night."

Fitch didn't offer his opinion on the likelihood of that.

"Do you want the money or don't you?"

Fitch took it.

He probably assumed he'd find dead bodies in the cottage. Lylene was too drained to wonder how he would sort it out. Desperate people, he probably thought them. Some desperate people. She settled herself behind Shile. No doubt Shile thought she hadn't noticed him slipping some of the real pennies in with the group of made ones he had given Fitch. And Weiland, swinging up onto his bay and scowling at her for watching him: She'd seen him leave one of his knives on the table—a finely honed blade in a village where iron was scant. She, still dressed in borrowed shirt and breeches, had left her dress, the only thing she had of her own.

Desperate people.

They were pathetic. How would they ever stand up to Theron?

15

For part of the journey she rode with Shile, who tried to cheer her with humorous tales and had no way of knowing that the story he started off with, the one about the thieving monk, was the same Jerel and Duncan had told her yesterday.

The rides behind Weiland were a different matter entirely. No idle chatter here: Twice he told her to sit centered, and once, when they passed through a thickly wooded area, he warned her to watch her head. Still, he didn't seem short-tempered, and—considering the consequences if she *hadn't* ducked—he might in fact have been making an effort to be pleasant.

Perhaps, Lylene thought, just as he had gone up in her estimation when she learned there was something he was afraid of, it could be he thought better of her once he saw that she obviously hadn't intended for matters to end the way they had—that she wasn't a totally heartless wizard. She relived finding herself with her head on Weiland's lap after Newlin had been killed by their pursuers, and she was thankful that she was sitting behind Weiland, where he couldn't see her face go red. More likely than being concerned about whether she was heartless, she told herself, Weiland was just relieved that she wasn't as powerful a wizard as he had feared.

They stopped short of Cragsfall, though it was only afternoon. Saldemar was another half day beyond that, and they didn't want to arrive at dusk, when the gate would be most carefully guarded.

"What I think we should do," Shile said, "is rest here overnight. First thing in the morning, we'll go to Cragsfall to pick up the things we'll need, then we'll head off for Saldemar at our best speed. That way, if Theron's got anybody in Cragsfall, they won't be able to send word ahead of us."

"What," Weiland asked, "things that we'll need?"

"Disguises," Shile said. "Supplies. Accouterments for getting into Saldemar."

Weiland cursed.

"What?"

"Can't you keep it simple for once? Can't you just—"

"Weiland, Weiland—"

"Don't 'Weiland, Weiland' me. You *always*

make everything more complicated than it needs to be."

"No, I don't."

"You don't know when to let up. You construct these grandiose schemes which collapse under the sheer weight—"

"Name me once."

Weiland didn't need time to consider. "Five days ago when you tried to talk Humphrey—"

"Besides Humphrey."

"The tournament at Stafford."

"Well, Stafford—"

"London."

"Not—"

"Ridgeshire. Charbonne. Lincoln."

"Maybe a little—"

"How about *Wales,* Shile? Our trip to Wales wasn't 'a little' anything."

"You're upsetting the Lady Lylene."

As though Shile's comment hadn't been totally irrelevant, Weiland purred, "Then she can take the first watch," and turned his back on them.

In the end, it was Shile who took the first watch, saying that was no job for a lady. Lylene suspected that Weiland was secretly relieved, that he wouldn't have slept had she been on guard. Shile watched and Weiland slept, and she lay under a gnarled oak tree with her face to the stars, thinking the ache would keep her awake forever.

And she awoke when someone gave her a hard kick in the ribs.

She curled around the new, physical pain. A pointed weight pressed against her chest, just enough pressure to let her know not to move. It took several hard blinks for her eyes to adjust to the darkness, to follow the length of the sword to the man who held it. "Harkta," she spat.

"Hello, little housekeeper. Not quite the conjurer princess yet, but no longer exactly the conjurer hag. For such a noble and self-righteous creature, you've dropped quite a few years." The wizard turned his face slightly, looking beyond her, and said: "Don't even think of trying anything."

Lylene slid her gaze to what the wizard looked at: Weiland, who appeared to her to be sound asleep. But Harkta said: "Put your hands behind your head and sit up, as slow and easy as you can," and Weiland put his hands behind his head. "Easy," Harkta warned. "*She* will pay for any mistakes *you* make."

Weiland sat up, apparently slow and easy enough to please him.

"On your knees." Then, finally easing up on the sword: "Now you. Stand up."

Lylene brought her legs around. From this new position she could see what would have been visible to Weiland all along: Shile, an untidy sprawl on the ground. *Please, not again,* she thought. Not someone else dead because of her.

"Stand up." Harkta slapped her arm with the flat edge of the sword.

She stood.

With his free hand the wizard tossed something at her. She flinched, but it was only a length of rope.

"Pick it up." Harkta spoke as though to a tiresome child. "Tie your friend's hands behind his back. And be advised: For every knot that isn't secure, I'm going to cut off one of your crooked little fingers." He leaned his left arm on a low-slung branch of the oak tree, comfortable and poised.

Lylene knelt behind Weiland.

"No talking," Harkta warned before she could get her mouth open.

She tied Weiland's wrists as loosely as she dared, which wasn't very loose at all, and waited for some sign, some signal to let her know what to do. If Weiland gave one, she missed it.

"Now your other young friend." Harkta tossed another length of rope at her.

At least he wasn't dead, which was what she'd feared. He groaned at her touch but didn't awaken. There was a large bump at the base of his skull, evidence that Harkta had come up behind him with sword hilt or rock. She pulled his limp arms behind his back and tied them there.

When she looked up, the wizard was checking Weiland's bonds. He jerked the sword, motioning her away from Shile and down on her knees between the two mercenaries. He examined Shile's bonds, then went back to his pose by the tree.

"I guess you can keep your fingers after all," he said with that boyish smile she remembered. "You've been busy. I understand you're responsible for killing off enough people to populate a small fishing village." His teeth flashed in the moonlight.

His words stung, too close to what she knew as truth.

"Witch, they call you," he continued, "the Demon Woman of Dorstede, who sucks souls from living men and steals children away into the night. They say a man who looks you in the eye is doomed to die within the hour. I alone have known your power and lived. I must say: You've enhanced my reputation enormously, and I *am* grateful."

"Vile buffoon," she said. "Without your magic you're a pasty-skinned toad."

His air of urbane aloofness vanished. Nostrils flared, eyes narrowed, and he took a step forward of the tree, his hand raised to slap her.

"Strike me," she dared. "Go ahead, touch me for one instant and see who comes out the worse."

That sobered him. He backed off. "You're *old,*" he taunted instead. "You're old, and you're soft, and you're very, very stupid. And Lord Theron is waiting to meet you."

Beside her, Shile stirred and groaned. He'd probably have a headache for the next two days.

Harkta's attention wavered from Lylene to Shile, back to Lylene, then snapped to Weiland, who had leaned backward onto his heels as the wizard glanced away. "Lord Theron might pay for the famous witch," Harkta said. "You I'm bringing back out of forbearance. Don't try me."

"Just a cramp," Weiland said, wide-eyed and guileless.

Lylene didn't believe that act for an instant, and neither did Harkta. "Turn around," he said shrilly. "Let me see those bindings again. *Now.*" He raised the sword but was reluctant to get close enough to use it.

"Easy," Weiland urged, the calm voice of reason. Was there the signal for which she had been waiting? She thought of Arandell, the Happy Wench, and the barkeep Marsh, killed by a knife Weiland had pulled from nowhere. Weiland turned on his knees, moving slowly, awkwardly, which was not like him at all, putting his back to her before Harkta. There was no time to make sure in the dim light. She turned to her right, to the still half-conscious Shile and screamed, "No, Shile, don't!"

Harkta jumped, swung toward Shile for the merest instant, probably realizing his mistake even as he made it.

Lylene heard him cry out. She turned in time to see him drop the sword and clap his left hand to the opposite shoulder, from which blood welled out.

Weiland was on his feet already, strands of cut rope falling loose from his wrists. The wizard's attention was all on the knife in his shoulder, and he made no attempt to defend himself. Weiland collided with him, slamming him into the trunk of the old oak. His left arm jammed against the wizard's windpipe, and his knee jerked up into his groin.

Harkta gave a strangled gurgle, and his eyes rolled upward.

Weiland ripped his knife out of the wizard's shoulder and swung it toward his belly.

Lylene recoiled, stunned by the savagery—no matter that it was directed against the treacherous Harkta—but Weiland checked the momentum of the knife just short of the wizard's mid-section, and finally eased up on Harkta's throat.

Harkta sucked in deep rattling breaths. "Damn . . . murderous . . . gutter trash," he wheezed. "Can't you see . . . I'm bleeding to death?" His eyelids fluttered and he started a slow downward slide, but Weiland left the knife where it was. Apparently Harkta wasn't so far gone that he didn't realize he was about to impale himself. He pulled himself back up and pressed against the tree, gasping.

No more than two handspans from Harkta's face, on the branch on which he had earlier been leaning, there was movement. For a moment, Lylene thought it was nothing: night shadows, breeze on loose bark. The movement slithered closer to Weiland's arm and flicked its tongue out to taste the air.

Icy revulsion fingered her back and arms. The snake was big—almost as wide around as her arm, its length lost in the shadows of the branches—and fast. Already it was within striking distance of Weiland. And still he hadn't seen it. She realized that she'd taken an instinctive step away and hated herself for it, for having thought of herself first. Her throat had constricted on itself, squeezing in the warning that she wanted to shout.

In that moment—battered by fear and guilt and self-loathing—it struck her how lucky Harkta was to get such a distraction at such a time.

Her throat relaxed somewhat, and she put her hand on Weiland's arm, the arm close to the snake. If she was wrong, at least she wouldn't live to regret it. "His specialty is illusion," she reminded him.

Weiland followed her gaze to the brown and gold snake. It had reared up and was swaying, its eyes on Weiland. For a moment Weiland just looked, no discernible expression on his face. What if he thought it was a real snake and, startled, let the wizard get away? What if he thought it was just an illusion, and it wasn't? What if—

Weiland slammed the wizard against the tree. "All right. That's it. I'm going to kill him."

The snake lunged.

Lylene screamed.

Weiland trusted her first inclination. He stayed where he was and hit the wizard across the face.

The snake disappeared.

"Don't kill me," Harkta begged. "Please. I swear: no more tricks. On my honor. Don't hurt me. I can help you."

Weiland glanced at her. "What do you think?"

This was a new game, asking her opinion. Did he want her permission to kill Harkta? Or an excuse not to? He and Shile knew each other, knew what to do and what to say in this sort of situation. She didn't know what was expected of her. "I . . ."

Next to her, Shile groaned yet again.

"Do you have a knife to cut his rope?" Weiland asked.

"No," she answered.

Without lowering the blade he held against the wizard, Weiland pulled another from his left boot.

Shile lifted his face out of the grass as she sawed at the rope. "Don't worry," he mumbled, "I'll rescue you."

"That's all right," she said. The frayed rope snapped, and she helped him sit up. "Easy now."

He rubbed the back of his head. "What are you doing?" he asked Weiland. "Are you tormenting that poor fellow for a particular purpose or just for the fun of it?"

"Yes," Weiland said.

Shile kept rubbing his head, then finally stood up, supporting his weight on Lylene's arm. "Theron?" he guessed.

"The Lady's wizard."

"Pity. Would have saved a lot of trouble if he was Theron. Is he likely to bleed to death in the immediate future?"

"Yes," Harkta moaned at the same time Weiland said, "No."

Shile approached, and the wizard backed right up against the tree. "Now, now," Shile told him, "don't be afraid of me. Just because you tried to crack my head open like a walnut doesn't mean I'm necessarily going to retaliate."

But Harkta wasn't even noticing him. All his attention focused on Lylene, and if he could have pushed himself into the tree, it was obvious he would have. "Don't," he said. Then to the others: "Don't let her touch me. I'll do whatever you want, tell you whatever you want. Just keep her away from me."

"Oh, I like the sound of this." Weiland grabbed the neck of Harkta's shirt and swung him around and down, so that he was kneeling at Lylene's feet.

Harkta had his eyes closed. "Don't touch me!" he begged.

And Lylene, with her hand reaching out, stopped, knowing that if she gave Harkta her extra years, he'd shed them on the first poor unfortunate he could touch. She let her hand drop to her side. He had been partly right: She didn't suck souls or steal children, but she had caused grief enough already.

Whatever Weiland was expecting, he looked bitterly disappointed.

Shile took over. "You work for Theron?" he asked.

"No," Harkta said.

Weiland said nothing, just rested his knife, flat side down, on the wizard's shoulder.

"That is—I mean—not generally."

"Tonight, specifically?" Shile asked.

"I Saw you coming. Word came about what happened in Arandell, so I cast about, Saw the three of you."

"Future-seeing?" Shile asked, looking to Lylene for confirmation.

She nodded.

Harkta glanced at her nervously. "I Saw you would go to Saldemar, so I went to Lord Theron. It's not that we're friends"—again the glance at Lylene—"but I thought he'd pay for the warning."

"You saw us going to Saldemar," Weiland said, moving the knife closer to Harkta's neck, so that the wizard had to tip his head back to keep from getting cut, "but you didn't see me disemboweling you and throwing the little pieces to the wolves?"

Harkta closed his eyes, and Shile silently mouthed, *Wolves?* for it was too late in the season for wolves to be this far south. Weiland shrugged.

"He can't see those parts of the future that involve him," Lylene explained.

Shile chewed on his lip. "But you could see us reaching Saldemar?"

Harkta started to nod, felt the knife against his skin, and whispered weakly: "Yes."

"And? Do we succeed in rescuing the Lady Lylene's sister from Theron?"

Harkta hesitated and Weiland, still holding onto the front of his shirt, twisted.

"No," Harkta answered. "You don't."

Lylene was sure her heart stopped beating. Weiland looked up, meeting her eyes. She turned her face, swallowed away the buzzing in her ears, felt the warmth of Shile's hand on her wrist. The moment passed.

"Liar," Weiland said. He let go of Harkta's shirt and jerked his head back by the hair.

"No." Lylene would have never guessed she'd say *no* to someone killing Harkta. "No, I don't think he can lie about the future." She shook her head for emphasis. "It's part of his magic."

"The future," Shile said thoughtfully, "can't be a stable thing?" He said it like a question. "It must be fluid, moving. Endless possibilities affected by endless possibilities."

"What?" Lylene asked testily. *Oh, Beryl,* she thought. All this for nothing?

"He's said we go to Saldemar and don't succeed. That's one possibility. Now that we know that, what if we don't go to Saldemar? That's another possibility, another future, and already different from the one he's foreseen. *What if we go to Saldemar forewarned?*"

Lylene swallowed hard again.

Weiland released Harkta's hair. "What exactly do you foresee, wizard?" he asked between clenched teeth.

"Ease off," Shile murmured. "You're scaring him so much he can't think."

Weiland shoved Harkta's head away from him and stepped back.

Harkta put his hand to his bloody shoulder and glowered. Then his lip curled back in a sneer. "You don't believe me? You want to help her? Go ahead. But *you*"—he pointed at Weiland—"if you go in there, you must be prepared to die."

Again the cold came up from the ground and seeped into Lylene.

Weiland never flinched or blanched. He stepped forward and put the knife to Harkta's throat again. "How are you at self-resurrections?"

"Leave him," Shile said. He, at least, looked properly shaken. He got a rope from his pack and bound Harkta to the tree. "Do you have a horse nearby?" he asked the wizard.

"Just over the hill."

"You alone? Or am I likely to meet anyone?"

"I told you: I went to Saldemar to warn Theron she was coming. Theron's not in the habit of providing me with escort. He even skimped on the payment. He wasn't terribly impressed with my news." He glanced at Lylene. "He didn't care. Said you were a pathetic *child* and you could come if you wanted. I wouldn't even be here except that I decided to stop for some herbs I'd been needing. Then I saw you."

"Then you saw us." Shile rubbed the back of his neck. "I'll get the horse," he told Lylene and Weiland. "If he gives you any trouble, go ahead and slice him up for the wolves."

Weiland gave a feral grin and got his sword from beside his bedroll. He unsheathed the blade, letting it scrape noisily along its great length, then he crouched down in front of Harkta, the naked blade across his knees.

"I'll bleed to death by the time he gets back," Harkta complained, trying to look pathetic.

Weiland shrugged.

"Half that blood is illusion," Lylene told Weiland. "The wound's not that bad at all."

Weiland didn't appear interested, one way or the other.

Lylene went to search for something to stanch the bleeding. The only thing she found was a red handkerchief in Shile's saddlebag, the original of the one Duncan had worn. She almost stuffed it back in.

After fixing the cloth about the wizard's shoulder, she crouched next to Weiland, resting her chin on her hands, watching, waiting.

Harkta's eyes darted from one to the other of them. "Damn it, I kept my part of the bargain. You got your magic, and I was willing to teach you how to use it. But you got all upset about the age thing. I explained that to you. If you kill me, you'll never learn. Lylene. Lylene, you know I've always had a soft spot in my heart for you."

"Shall we hug and make up?" she asked.

He licked his lips. "You don't know how to use your magic properly. Those human duplicates you made—"

Her breath caught.

"—I Saw that. You went about it all wrong. It doesn't have to be like that. You put too much power in it, too much concentration. All you want is a . . . a likeness, a fetch, just a mindless, soulless—"

"Shut up."

Weiland was silently taking all this in.

"No harm," Harkta said. "Really. To you or your friends. I can show you how. You can go on making duplicates of them indefinitely, and it won't hurt anyone."

She covered her ears.

Weiland stood.

"No!" Harkta cried, cringing.

Weiland slammed the sword back into its sheath. "Damn," he muttered.

Beyond Harkta, Shile was approaching, leading Harkta's horse. He motioned Lylene and Weiland to leave Harkta under the tree and moved beyond his range of hearing. "Well," he said to them, "so what do you think?"

"About *what?*" Weiland asked, never a patient man.

"Plans for breaching Saldemar."

"Shile, weren't you listening—"

"I was listening. I have my doubts."

"You . . ." Weiland gave up without saying anything. He turned to Lylene. "I'm sorry," he said. "I am not willing to die for you. You or your sister."

She could understand that. But Shile cut her off before she could answer. "I can see how you feel that way," he told Weiland.

"And don't talk to me in that—"

"You keep a watch on the wizard. The Lady and I will rescue the sister."

Weiland shook his head in disbelief, but this time it was Lylene who got her voice to work first: "No. This isn't your affair."

"Of course it is," Shile said. "You hired us."

"Then I'm releasing you. It's too dangerous."

"You'd leave your sister to her fate?"

"I'll . . . come up with a new plan."

"My Lady—"

"He said the rescue wouldn't work. He said Weiland would die."

"I don't believe it, and anyway—"

"I do believe it. Shile, he's clever, he's treacherous, but he can't lie about what he Sees. I *did* learn something during my stay with him."

"Well, it's on that chance that we're leaving Weiland here."

"Shile—" Weiland started.

"Weiland," Shile said. "My Lady. I will go."

"Shile," Weiland pleaded. "Wizardry is too dangerous to—"

"Just wait here," Shile said. "This wizard . . . Weiland, this wizard can make us a fortune."

"Damn it, *listen to me.*"

"No. No, I will not. For once would you just listen to me? With no arguing, no grumbling—"

"Shile, you're an idiot." Weiland hooked sword onto harness and stalked away. He grabbed up his saddle kit and headed for his horse. "You want the wizard, you watch him. I'm not waiting around."

Lylene looked from Weiland's retreating back to Shile to Weiland. "Weiland," she called, because Shile was going to let him go.

But Weiland didn't turn back. They had left the horses' equipment on loosely, and it took him only a moment to tighten and check, and then he swung on.

"You're not just going to let him go?" Lylene demanded of Shile.

But he did.

16

Shile crouched by the dying embers of the campfire, trying to catch enough light to read the paper he held. The sun was just visible over the horizon, casting a pink glow over everything. Lylene stooped next to him.

"Map of Saldemar," he explained, though that wasn't what she wanted to talk about. "Weiland drew it yesterday evening while you were . . . resting."

"Oh, Shile, I'm so sorry—"

"Don't worry. He'll be back."

His confidence was reassuring. "He's . . . walked out before?"

Shile hesitated.

"Shile, I'm sorry. You're partners. I didn't mean to come between you." She didn't add that Weiland was the one who was more likely to keep his feet firmly on the ground.

"Shhh. It's all right. Probably safer this way. Though I'm still not convinced that wizard of yours is being honest with us. Weiland's real skittish when it comes to magic. We'll find him after we finish this job." He patted her hand and went back to studying the map.

"Speaking of that wizard . . ."

Shile looked up again.

"What are we going to do with him?"

"Take him with us, of course."

"You can't be serious. He'll turn on us the first chance he gets."

Shile shook his head.

"Shile, he's dangerous."

"But controllable."

Lylene couldn't believe they were even arguing about this. "How?"

"With a knife to his ribs."

Lylene rested her chin on her palm, watching Harkta. "I don't know: I kind of liked the plan with the wolves."

The wizard sat in a pathetic slump, pretending he couldn't hear.

Shile said: "Besides, with his ability to cast illusions he can disguise us."

"Why? Theron doesn't know either of us."

"Someone in his employ may have seen me before."

She sighed. Cheating at cards or picking purses, probably.

"Or—more likely—might recognize you as the aggrieved sister."

She suspected he just liked disguises. "We can be disguised without him," she pointed out. "Shile—"

"Tell you what . . ." He pulled a coin from his pocket.

"No, this isn't the kind of thing to be settled with a coin toss."

"It's exactly the kind of thing to be settled with a coin toss. A difference of opinion. Neither party able to convince the other. No compromise possible. Look," he showed her the ancient gold coin, worn almost to obliteration, "on this side, His Royal Highness King Something-or-other of Phoenicia. On this side . . . looks like a god who bears an uncanny resemblance to a fish-eyed falcon. Pick a side."

Being a devout Christian, she felt obliged to select the king.

"All right," Shile said: "God, we have Harkta get us inside Saldemar; king, you come up with another plan."

"But—"

It didn't make any difference: The coin landed god's face up.

Shile grinned, pocketing the coin.

Harkta. She hoped Shile knew what he was doing. "All right. What's he going to disguise us as?"

Shile thought about it for a moment. "Glaziers."

"Glaziers?"

"We'll say Theron has hired us to fit the windows with glass. It's the latest fashion. To please his pretty new wife." Shile caught himself. "My Lady, I'm sorry. Sometimes my mouth . . ."

She considered. "It might work. If Theron did want glass, it'd be in the living quarters. So we'd have an excuse to be wandering around there."

"The west tower. That's what Weiland said." He raised his voice for Harkta. "Can you do it, wizard?" He pulled a knife from his belt and flipped it in the air, catching it by the handle, a trick she'd be willing to bet Weiland had taught him. "Horses and all?"

Harkta nodded.

"Show us."

Shile's features shimmered, shifted. He was suddenly bald, with a round, florid face. Harkta had a gray beard and a bulbous nose. Lylene looked down and saw that her chest was flat, though broad, and her hands large and calloused: a man, a young laborer. Shile's horse was a dappled gray mare, and Harkta's a light brown one, working men's horses.

Maybe, she thought. *If*— She fought not to think of all the *ifs,* to hold on to the maybe. Maybe.

It was still early morning when they reached Saldemar. Just before cresting the last hill, Shile had to untie Harkta. For this they switched horses. Lylene got Harkta's, which was still a large, restive gelding, no matter what it looked like, and just about all she could handle. Shile sat behind Harkta on the horse that seemed to be a dappled mare. From the expression on the wizard's face, Shile had been serious about keeping a knife to his ribs.

Saldemar was no bigger than Delroy, but much better fortified. There were lookout towers in good repair, a gatehouse which probably included a portcullis, and the walls were heavily crenellated and looped for archers. The whole structure sat on a hill and was surrounded by a moat.

"Everyone," Shile said, "keep calm, act natural. Wizard, twitch and you die."

At the outer gate, Shile talked loud and fast, and the guards waved them into the barbican.

Lylene dismounted, bumping one of the guards, then the other, leaving each a year older. Anyone who worked for Theron, she reasoned, had probably done more than enough to deserve it. She caught Shile glancing upward, and she did likewise. She'd been right to worry about the portcullis. That would come down at the first hint of something amiss—locking those who were out, out, and those who were in—if they didn't belong in—would be in serious trouble.

At the stable, there was a dice game going on the floor.

Make your wager, hope for the best, and throw, she thought. She walked around the circle, studying several throws, leaning here, resting a hand there, accidentally stepping on toes. She began to get dirty looks.

Shile hissed in her ear: "You're affecting the illusion Harkta made for you. You're making your disguise younger." He motioned with his head for her to leave. He followed Harkta, close enough to step on his heels as they climbed the stairs to the entrance of the keep itself.

"Glaziers," Shile said, shoving Harkta in through the doorway, "come to measure."

The guard shoved them back out. "I don't know nothing about no glaziers."

"Nobody seems to," Shile complained. "We had trouble at the gate, too. Lord Theron hired us."

"Didn't tell me about it."

"Oh. Well then. Obviously. If he didn't discuss it with you . . . You can't be too careful about rogue craftsmen coming in and doing all sorts of work for free."

The guard scowled.

"Go on, go call Lord Theron away from whatever it is he's doing. He's a patient man, I understand. Just make sure you tell him it was *you* who wanted to know."

The guard sucked on his teeth. "Well, I think it'll be all right then."

"Are you sure? You might want to demand that Lord Theron come all the way over here to tell you it's all right."

Lylene kicked his heel.

"No," the guard said slowly. "I guess it'll be all right."

"I thank you," Shile said. "My assistants thank you. My poor dead father—"

Lylene pushed Shile, and Shile pushed Harkta, and they were inside the castle. "You don't know when to stop, do you?" she demanded in a harsh whisper. Weiland was right.

"We don't want him with any lingering doubts. Let's see, if I remember correctly—"

A squad of soldiers came around a corner, looking more sharp and alert than those with whom they had dealt so far. Shile tugged Harkta to the side to let them pass.

And Harkta burst into flame.

With a startled oath, Shile jumped back, letting go of him.

"No!" Lylene cried. No heat, no burning, but it happened so fast she couldn't blame Shile for reacting instinctively.

And by then they had all reverted back to their real forms, and Harkta was screaming, "Arrest them! Arrest them! Arrest them!"

In an instant, the men had their swords out.

Shile, just going for his, stopped and left his hands where the guards could see them.

The guard who'd been in the lead grabbed Harkta by the front of his shirt. "Don't you give orders to my men, wizard," he snarled.

"These are the ones!" Harkta insisted.

The man looked down at the wizard coolly until Harkta spoke more calmly.

"Sorry, Sir Owen. But these are the people I was telling Lord Theron about, the ones who've been threatening him, that were going to break into Saldemar."

"I see. That's why you led them in."

Harkta twitched a smile. "Into your capable hands, Owen, as captain of the guard."

"You always have an answer, wizard." The captain shoved him away. "Go," he said to one of his men. "Take him to see Theron." And to another: "Disarm them."

The man took Shile's sword and dagger, then patted his hands up and down Lylene's body. She got through it by telling herself that—bad as it was—at least he took no liberties. Apparently this Owen had his charges under strict control.

"Nothing, sir."

Owen looked at Shile. "So," he said. And grinned. "Weiland's friend."

"I was about to say the same."

"Then you would have said wrong. Where is he?"

Shile shook his head. "Didn't come."

"I don't blame him. Harkta said you were coming. Said why. I found it hard to believe Weiland'd be stupid enough to come back. Especially for a whore." He glanced at Lylene, and she felt her cheeks go red, that he would think that of her.

"Owen," Shile said, "I know Weiland always thought of you as a friend and was very sorry—"

"No," Owen interrupted, hand upraised. "Please. Don't. Let's have some respect for each other, shall we? I liked Weiland. I considered him a friend. He showed a lot of promise, and I recommended him for promotion. When he walked off with half the year's tax monies—during my watch . . ." Owen shook his head. ". . . I don't think he was looking back and feeling sorry."

The guard who had taken Harkta to see Theron came back. "Says to put 'em down in the dungeon until he's got the time to question them."

At least he didn't order us killed out of hand, Lylene thought. But it was hard to find comfort in that.

Owen and his guards brought them down an incredibly steep set of stairs with a heavy oak door at the bottom.

Someone on the other side opened a tiny metal door set at eye level.

"Prisoners," Owen announced.

The metal peephole slammed shut, and the wooden door opened. There were two guards down here. One of them led their group down a corridor, passing through another locked door.

The cell, when they finally got to it, was small, the walls rough and crumbly, and it smelled damp. It was also dark, as she discovered when the door slammed shut on them.

The dungeon guard worked the metal window back and forth to ease the rusty hinge. "This is where you'll get your food," he said. "If anybody authorizes food for you." He slammed it shut again.

In the dark, something brushed against her hand. She snatched it away with a startled squeak.

"Just me," Shile said.

She felt for his hand, and he squeezed reassuringly. "My eyes haven't adjusted yet," she said.

"I don't think they will: It's too dark. I think we better sit. On the count of three: one, two, three."

They sat.

And he was right.

Their eyes didn't adjust.

17

Lylene was disconcerted that her surroundings got no blacker when she shut her eyes. She listened to the steady drip of water from somewhere behind their cell, and to the little rustling noises which came from every direction. She tried to convince herself that rats were the least of her worries.

Shile had nothing to say for the longest time.

Occasionally a far-off door slammed, bringing a snatch of conversation on an air current, the words indecipherable.

Hours passed. Lylene felt the stir of a draft around her ankles. She raised her head and swallowed hard. Shile squeezed her hand.

Voices approached, still indistinct. Laughter. The creak of hinges straining under a heavy weight. The dark lessened. Not brightness, but now there was a difference between eyes open and eyes closed.

Footsteps. The jangle of mail. A shaft of light

appeared underneath the door of their cell. Tiny red eyes close to the floor were caught in that light, blinked in surprise, then disappeared into a crack in the wall.

"This them?" The voice was slurred and unsteady. "Are you the dangerous prisoners?"

Laughter. "You idiot. I haven't opened the peephole yet."

"Could of sworn I saw 'em. Two—s'cuse me—two big, hairy brutes."

Shadows danced under their door as the guards outside—three or four of them by the noise they made—stumbled around with their torches. It sounded as if they all had been drinking.

Shile slumped back down, his interest gone.

Muffled giggling, then a new voice said: "Damnation, that's some strong ale you brought. What's in it?"

"Wizards' blood and wolf piss," the first voice answered. "Want some more?"

Apparently he did. Apparently they all did.

Lylene rocked back and forth. Obviously these weren't sent by Theron to fetch them or question them. They probably weren't even supposed to be here. She just hoped they weren't so drunk they'd try anything on their own. She hadn't appreciated before how lucky they'd been with Owen.

She put her head down on her knees, so that

only her hair would show. Hopefully the grayness of it would keep the men from being interested. She appeared in her forties now, and that wasn't so very old that it would protect her.

"So." It was the first man again. "So, where are they?"

The little door in front of the barred window was flung open, flooding the cell with torchlight.

"Hey. Hey, dangerous prisoners. Le'see your faces."

Lylene screwed her eyes shut and prayed they'd go away.

"They look—s'cuse me—they look like they're friends."

One of the others snorted.

"S'good to have friends," the first insisted. "Specially when one is indis . . . posed. Isen it? Isen it nice to have friends?"

The words were uncannily familiar. A tingle began at the base of Lylene's spine and went up all the way to the tips of her hair. Shile had said that, or something very like it, outside the Happy Wench. Playing the drunk. A disguise of sorts. Slowly, not daring to hope, she raised her head.

Four faces crowded together around a torch to peer into their barred window. Guards, all wearing helmets, their faces made similar by no hair showing, by the noseguards, and by the flickering torch.

She didn't have to look past the second one on the right.

"Well"—how could she not have recognized Weiland's voice, despite the drunken slur?—"you'ere right about one thing: She ain't no big hairy brute."

Lylene stole a glance at Shile, who sat in a disconsolate slump, staring at the tips of his boots, ignoring everything. She nudged him. He ignored that too.

The man on Weiland's left punched his shoulder amicably. "Not so dangerous, not so interesting. Come on, lad, let's go have some more of that ale you brung."

Weiland's blue eyes shifted back and forth between her and Shile.

She moved her foot, kicking Shile's leg, but that seemed to drive him even deeper into his own thoughts.

One of the others had already turned to go, and the man on Weiland's left said again, "Come on."

Her arms were still wrapped around her knees. She reached her left hand under her right arm and, as hard as she could, pinched the inside of Shile's thigh.

That got his attention.

"Now that one," Weiland said, abandoning

as much of the drunken slur as he dared, "*is* a big, hairy brute."

Shile looked up.

Weiland pushed himself away from the grate.

"Hey!" Shile bellowed. "You! Swine-breath!"

Trouble: The other three guards made appreciative noises and turned back.

Weiland pointed to himself, incredulous. "Me? Are you talking to me?"

Shile scrambled to his feet. "No, I'm talking to your mother. Of course, I'm talking to you, you stupid oaf."

Lylene got up also, to be ready for whatever was coming.

Weiland pulled his sword and staggered forward. "Just be thankful this door is between us."

Shile stepped closer. "Scare me some more."

"Back off," one of the guards warned him, the one who held the torch. "Keep away from the door."

"I'm going to volunteer for your execution," Weiland said, raising his sword. Then, turning to the others: "Let's drink to that."

"Good thinking, lad." Two of the guards started moving down the corridor to the guardroom. The last reached to close their window opening. Weiland swung the sword around, cutting deep into his back. The man dropped without uttering a sound, but the remaining guards heard the thud of metal on flesh. As if that weren't warning enough, the slain guard's torch fell to the floor, still burning, sending bizarre shadows dancing on the walls.

One swore.

The other didn't.

They both had their swords out faster than Lylene would have believed.

Weiland moved fast too. Swords came together, scraped, came together again. Weiland circled around, so that they had their backs to the cell door. He lunged, which seemed folly, but one of the guards took a step backward.

Weiland darted back, and Shile, waiting by the grate, grabbed the collar of the guard who had come too close. He slammed him into the door, then shoved him away, then slammed him again. He repeated the back and forth movement three more times before he let go, and the man slid down and out of sight.

The sounds of fighting in the corridor had stopped.

Shile turned to wink at Lylene. She stepped closer to the window grating. Three bodies on the floor and Weiland taking the keys off one of them. She concentrated on him, on his welcome face, and tried to avoid taking in the bloody bodies. It was her doing, all of this.

"I was sure you'd come," Shile said.

"*I* wasn't sure I'd come," Weiland objected. But then he said, "They were talking in town about an execution planned for tomorrow, and I figured that had to be you." He got the door open and Shile flung his arm around him, almost toppling him.

Lylene would have hugged him, too, if she could have been sure of his reaction.

"How'd you get in?" Shile asked.

"Asked if they were hiring men and walked in."

Shile, no doubt remembering their disguises, sighed.

Weiland looked at Lylene appraisingly. She had taken off eight years since last night. "This life suits you," he observed dryly.

Was "thank you" appropriate under the circumstances?

Shile's dark eyes went from one to the other. "We better talk about a new plan. Weiland, we've lost track of the time—is it night yet?"

"Not quite supper."

"All right, it'd probably be safest to wait here until everyone goes to bed—"

"Watch'll change before then."

Shile stooped to loosen the sword belt from one of the guards. "We appreciate the timely rescue," he said, "but maybe a few more hours—"

"I talked to the guards who were going to be coming on. Their captain didn't seem one to take any nonsense. I didn't think I could talk him into letting me in, free ale or not."

Lylene, about to ask how he had come by the ale, decided she probably didn't want to know.

Shile looked up from taking a helmet. "My Lady, I'm afraid we'll have to make a guard out of you." He put one of the sword belts in her hand.

"I can't . . . I'll never pass—"

"Try it."

"Shile—"

"Try it."

"Be reasonable."

He reached into his pocket. "King, we do it my way; god, you come up with a plan."

"Shile—" she started as Shile flipped the old coin into the air.

Weiland caught it mid-spin and broke into a stream of profanity.

"What?" Lylene asked. "What is it?"

"Has he tried this before?"

She glanced at Shile.

"He knows how to control it. Nine times out of ten he can make it land on the side he's called."

"That's not possible." But Shile's face told her it was. "Blackguard," she said. "Cheater."

"Well," Shile said, "yes."

Weiland handed her the coin. "If you need it to make decisions, *you* do the flipping."

She nodded.

"But for now . . ." Weiland took the belt and fastened it around her waist. "We won't get out of here otherwise."

Shile put one of the helmets on her head. It smelled of stale sweat and slipped down almost to her eyes, with the noseguard overlapping her upper lip.

"Put your hair up," Weiland suggested. "That'll hide it and make for a snugger fit."

He must have done something of the sort also, for his distinctive blond hair didn't show. She made a quick braid. The helmet still smelled, but the fit was better.

Shile said: "If anyone asks, we're heading for the west tower—sent to help in a matter of some particularly audacious rats which have been terrorizing the women." He turned suddenly. "We met that friend of yours."

"Owen," Lylene said.

No telling from Weiland's expression what he thought of that.

As they passed through the guardroom, he suddenly turned to Lylene. "Here"—he had pulled a sheathed dagger from who-knew-where and held it out to her—"the sword's just for show. You'll need a weapon you won't kill yourself trying to use."

She hesitated. "Thank you."

Weiland made a sound of contempt. "Take it out and see if the handle's comfortable."

She slipped the blade partially from its sheath. "It's fine. Thank you."

Weiland snatched the weapon out of her hand and hooked it onto her belt before she had a chance to protest that she could manage herself. "Lady, is this a game to you, or what?"

"Leave her alone, Weiland," Shile said.

"No," Lylene said to Weiland. "This is no game."

Shile made to move between them, but she just raised her voice. "I don't know what you expect of me. I was raised—" She knew it'd be better not to say it but couldn't help herself. "I was raised in polite company." That was to hurt Weiland, who she suspected couldn't say the same. But his expression never changed. "My parents didn't think to teach us how to use daggers and swords. But when my sister was stolen away, I vowed to fight back. I've lied and cheated people and hurt them and done so many shameful things, I can't even remember them all. And the thing is . . . the thing is I'm not used to all this. *You* tell me what to do, you point me in the right direction, and when the time comes I'll take this knife and slit Theron's throat with it."

Weiland looked openly skeptical.

"I'm not going to back down or hamper you: I shall kill Theron."

She could tell by Shile's face that she had said

the wrong thing, that she had touched on something Weiland wasn't going to let pass.

Weiland said, "You stubborn, arrogant—"

"*Me?*" Of all the people to accuse her of that—and just when she'd been letting herself start to like him—

"—self-centered—"

"Weiland," Shile begged, "leave it."

Weiland shrugged out from under his hand. "'I will, I shall, I can.' Since when do you have the gift of prophecy? Things are *never* what you presume. You *presume* you know how you'll handle some situation, but it's never exactly the situation you're prepared for. You say, 'If that'd been me' or 'I'd never have done that,' but then it happens so fast, or someone's there with you, or nobody's there, or something's different, and your *presumptions* about yourself are wrong, and there you are with no one else to blame and all the rest of your life to regret it." Weiland sat down heavily on the table and crossed his arms across his chest, daring her to disagree.

Not Lylene. She had no idea what he was talking about, and at the same time she knew exactly what he was talking about.

Shile finally said, "Let us know when you're through."

Weiland continued to look down his nose at both of them for another few moments before standing. "I'm through."

"I'll take the lead," Shile said.

"You don't know your way around."

"You can tell me from behind."

It was to protect Weiland: Harkta's prophecy preyed on Shile's mind, no matter how he denied it—Weiland was the one in the greatest danger.

Lylene slowed so that Weiland had to either drop further behind and lose sight of Shile or catch up to her.

"The thing about regrets," she said, and this was new to her, too, "is that they don't change anything, and they eat away at you from the inside out until there's nothing left at all."

Weiland regarded her coldly for a moment. He lengthened his stride to close the gap Shile was forming. "I regret nothing," he said.

18

They only made it as far as the top of the stairs.

Lylene was puffing from the exertion—her added years were felt most keenly with stairs—and it was a long, steep climb that curved dizzyingly. They had just stepped through the doorway when a deep voice yelled: "Hey!"

Weiland swore under his breath, then pushed in front of Shile, muttering, "Frazier." To the guard, he said: "Sir?"

The man scowled at him, thumbs hooked into his sword belt. "You're the new man."

"Tearle," Weiland said.

"Yeah, Tearle. What were you doing down there?"

"Looking. Getting a feel for the lay of the place."

"You were shown around this afternoon."

"It's a big place."

The man wasn't sure. He inched his hand

closer to the sword hilt. His eyes shifted warily. "And who are these?"

Confidently, aggressively, Shile said: "Damn, Frazier, it's me—Garrett. Is your memory slipping, getting too old? And you've got to remember Dillon." He gave Lylene a good-natured punch on the arm.

The fact that they knew his name made Frazier hesitate, mistrust his instincts. His hand stayed by the sword, though. He returned his attention to Weiland. "So what is this: Your first day on the job, and they give you the night off? You all got the night off?"

"He's supposed to be on the western bartizan," Shile said, inclining his head toward Weiland, "but he never showed up. Captain Owen sent us to fetch him. We found him drinking and gaming with the downstairs crew. I don't think he's going to work out at all."

Frazier looked almost convinced. "They're hiring lackwits." He started toward the door. "I'd better check on the watch if they've been drinking."

"No," Shile said, too quickly. "*They* haven't. Just . . ." He had obviously forgotten the name Weiland had used and finished lamely, "him."

Frazier took them all in at a glance. "Oh." He stepped backward. "Well. So long as everything's all right."

Weiland went for his sword first, then Shile did.

Shile's hadn't cleared the scabbard when Frazier hit him in the face with his elbow, knocking him backward down the stairs. Part of the same movement: Frazier's fist slammed into Lylene above her heart. She felt her left foot go over the edge, skidding first off one step, then the next. She threw her weight forward so her right knee scraped the edge of the landing, but at least she broke her fall. Frazier kicked at her, hitting the crown of the helmet. It flew off and she heard it bouncing down the steep stairs.

He had drawn his sword now but turned to fend off Weiland.

She grabbed Frazier's leg and dragged on it with all her weight, distracting, putting him off balance.

Weiland slashed across his throat. Blood splattered Lylene, and then Frazier toppled. Weiland threw himself down to catch her arm before she had time to realize she was in danger. She let go of Frazier's leg, and he slid about halfway down the curved stairs before coming to rest against the wall.

Weiland leapt first over her, then over Frazier, hurtling down the stairs after Shile.

Lylene came two steps behind him all the way. "Sweet Saint Marcelle," she breathed, for the right side of Shile's face was bloody and his limbs were all at impossible angles.

Weiland knelt beside him, and she sank to her knees on the other side.

"Shile." Weiland leaned close and Shile's eyelids fluttered. More urgently: "Shile."

"S'alright," Shile muttered thickly, giving up on opening his eyes. "Doesn' hurt."

Which didn't sound good at all.

Weiland looked up at her, as though waiting for her—*her*—to tell him what to do.

She found Shile's hand, squeezed it.

He didn't respond at all. "Don' feel anything," he muttered. "Jus' dizzy. Jus' . . ."

She had to lean close to make sure that his chest was still moving, that he was still breathing, though common sense said that after the exertion of the fight and the fall, he should have been breathing hard, his chest heaving, as were hers and Weiland's.

Weiland leaned back on his heels. "He's dying."

She made a shushing motion. Shile didn't need to hear that.

"He's dying." His voice was flat, emotionless. Only his paleness belied her impression that he felt nothing.

She nodded, hating him anyway.

"Can your magic help?"

"No," she whispered.

He took a deep breath. "Then do whatever it is you do to become younger."

She looked at him in horror.

"In a couple moments he'll be dead, and it'll be too late." He reached over his dying partner to grab her arm, and she twisted away.

"Damn you," she said.

He took hold of her again, hard enough to hurt. "It won't make any difference to him, and it might help us get out of here alive."

"Let go of me."

"You're too old, you're too slow."

"Let go—"

He lunged to grab her gray braid at the nape of her neck and forced her down closer to the unconscious Shile. "Do it!"

She tugged at his fingers. "I hate you!"

"I don't care. Do it."

She could have transferred those years to Weiland. Perhaps he didn't realize that. Perhaps he trusted her not to.

She did consider it.

Instead, she took Shile's face in her hands and leaned to kiss his lips. She closed her eyes and saw him at the Happy Wench, watching her. *I'll help you,* his eyes said. Dark, sparkling eyes in which she'd seen loyalty and kindness.

She'd betrayed that once before, by creating Jerel and Duncan and Newlin.

There was no tingle this time, or perhaps she just didn't feel it. She opened her eyes. It was still Shile's face. But now the hair, except where it was plastered to his cheek with blood, was shot through with gray. The crinkles he'd always had at the corners of his eyes and mouth were exaggerated, and the cheeks were sunken. She caressed the sticky hair away from his cheek, and he sighed once. Then he didn't move again.

After a long while she looked up.

Weiland had let go of her; she hadn't noticed that. He must have got up and walked away, which she hadn't noticed either, for he was sitting now at the far side of the landing. He had taken off his helmet, and he sat—with his back to the wall and his knees drawn up to his chest—leaning forward, his face hidden.

She stood, wishing he'd died instead of Shile. Shile wouldn't have betrayed him. Shile wouldn't have betrayed either of them. Her braid fell in front of her shoulder, copper orange. Her hands were young, her face, the rest of her body. She'd be able to keep up now.

She pushed the braid back, and it was only that motion which made her notice there was something different about Weiland. He had taken off his helmet, but now she saw he hadn't braided or twisted his long hair to hide it—he had cut it off. Of course he'd have had to. He wouldn't have been wearing a helmet when he came to Saldemar, and that long hair, reminiscent of the Vikings, was too distinctive, would have been remembered from when he'd worked here before.

He looked up, his grimy face streaked with tears, which she hadn't expected. The roughly shorn hair and the tears made him look very young. He put his face in his hands, and his shoulders, shook hard enough she could see it from here.

She knelt next to him and he threw his arms around her. "It was supposed to be me," he said.

Which was when she remembered Harkta's prophecy was yet to be fulfilled.

19

"It was Shile always had the plans," Weiland said.

Lylene could sympathize with that. But it didn't help. "We have to get out of here. Out of the castle." Try again, she thought. Some other plan, some other people. God help her: Beryl had waited eight months, she could wait a few days more. "If we can hide someplace until tomorrow, until they open the gate—"

Weiland shook his head. "We'll finish it."

"Harkta said you'd die." Fear made her blunt.

"I'm already here. I might die trying to get out. I may as well die rescuing your sister."

It was hard to think, faced with that logic. "We have no plan," she reminded him.

Weiland talked slowly, considering. "They'll all be at supper now in the Great Hall. We'll go to her room, hide there till everyone's asleep, and then break out, the three of us."

"We can't just leave Shile," she said.

"Yes, we can."

She saw how much that cost and didn't argue.

It cost her, too.

He tossed her helmet to her, and they went up the stairs, ignoring the lifeless lump that had been Frazier.

Through passages they went, up stairs, across more passages, up more stairs. There were few servants about, but Lylene kept her head ducked down, just in case. It was in this stance that they rounded a corner and she almost bumped into a guard.

Weiland saluted, kept on walking. Lylene copied the gesture. Took one step beyond. Two. Three.

"You."

She closed her eyes, thinking, *Not again.*

"They finished downstairs yet?"

It took several thumping heartbeats to realize he meant supper and nothing to do with them or the dungeon.

Weiland said, "Who knows? We don't get our meal until we've checked for rats in the ladies' quarters."

"Rats?" the man repeated incredulously. He was eying Lylene, her blood-speckled shirt.

Weiland shrugged. "So the ladies say."

"Where, exactly?"

Beside her, she felt Weiland tense, about to

go for his sword. Not here, she thought. It was too close to Beryl's room. Blood and dead bodies up here would raise too much commotion.

A bell rang loudly, clamoring alarm.

"That's the signal for escaped prisoners," Weiland said. "You take these stairs. We'll circle round by the kitchens." He slapped Lylene's arm to get her moving, and the two of them sprinted toward the back stairs.

But they stopped as soon as they saw the guard had followed Weiland's instructions.

Lylene leaned against the wall, feeling weak.

Weiland grabbed her arm and pulled her back the way they had come. "Here," he whispered, stopping in front of one of the doors. He listened for movement within, then took a torch from its socket on the wall and cautiously eased open the door.

The room was empty, though lit already. It was a lady's dressing area, more ornate than she would have expected, with thick tapestries on the walls and furs strewn on the floor to protect dainty feet from morning chills. There was a table littered with glass jars of ointments and creams, tortiseshell combs, ivory trinkets. At least Theron knew what the apartments of a woman of gentle birth should be like.

Weiland looked at her with raised eyebrows, then moved silently toward the inner room, the sleeping bower. He eased the door open.

Three guards waited in the bedchamber, standing with armed crossbows pointed at them.

And Harkta lay sprawled on the bed. Grinning.

"Ah, the conjurer princess," he said. "And her consort. You certainly did take your time."

Weiland flung the torch.

It *whooshed* through the air, over the wizard's head and between and beyond two of the guards. All instinctively ducked. And the torch hit the tapestry-hung wall behind.

Lylene turned to flee.

Standing in front of her, a drawn sword not a fingerwidth from her bosom, was a fourth guard.

And Owen stood before Weiland, in similar pose.

Behind Lylene, Harkta swore. The guards tore down the tapestry. There was already the stench of burning—wool and the more acrid fur of the floor throwings. Lylene could hear the men stamping out the fire.

"Bells ringing," Owen said, "people shouting, alarms in the night, fire in the west tower: I would have known anywhere it was you, Weiland." Owen walked around him appraisingly, tapping the sword pensively on Weiland's shoulders.

Don't, Lylene prayed, *don't.*

"You see—" Harkta scrambled off the bed—"I was right. I told Lord Theron they'd come here. I told him."

"You told him," Owen acknowledged. "You almost botched the capture, but you told him."

Harkta glared at the captain's back, stung by his rebuke. He lashed out at Weiland: "Prepared to die, villein?"

"He's just a hireling," Lylene told Owen. He was the power here, no matter what Harkta thought. *Not Weiland, too*, she thought. Of all the deaths she had caused—at least three, of men far more innocent—she couldn't bear the thought of Weiland's blood on her hands. "He's not responsible. I am. Theron's quarrel is with me, not him."

"Interesting," Owen said. "Interesting development."

Weiland stared at the floor.

Harkta was still trying to act like the one in charge. "Tie his hands," he ordered. "Get her sword."

The men waited until Owen nodded assent.

"Look," Owen said, "wizard: I don't like you. Lord Theron doesn't like you. He tolerates you because . . . Actually I don't know why he tolerates you. You're a mealy-mouthed, treacherous little worm. So don't press your luck."

Harkta flushed with embarrassment. And again took it out on the prisoners. "Laugh," he told Lylene, though she hadn't. "Go ahead. You always were a stupid girl. Mistake after mistake after mistake. The first thing you did wrong—today—was you didn't even think to ask if both of your companions would die."

The breath she sucked in hurt all the way down.

"And second—second, you little ninny—you didn't even have the sense to use your hard-earned magical ability: You should have used fetches of them. Then it wouldn't have mattered if they had died."

Emotions fell over each other to get to the forefront. Guilt. Rage. Grief. Fear.

Rage won.

She gave a cry as of pain and covered her face with her hands. She made her shoulders shake and gave loud sobbing noises.

"Ninny," Harkta gloated, coming in closer. That was like him: He had to rub it in, especially after being humiliated by Owen. "You never learned to use your brain." He tapped his finger roughly against her head.

She grabbed his hand and wished.

The guard standing behind her swore and took a step away.

Even the normally steady Owen was startled. "What the hell is that?" He looked from one form of Harkta to the other.

"You . . . You . . . You . . ." said the one on

the left, the original, pointing at her, his face turning purple.

"How dare you?" the other demanded, a similar shade.

Weiland, his arms tied behind his back, gave her a wary glance that asked why they needed two Harktas.

"I want you to kill them," she said, without letting her eyes rest long on either Harkta. "I want you to kill all the guards, and Theron, too. Quick, look like you don't know what I'm talking about." It was pure fabrication, of course. The fetch was an exact replication of Harkta, with all of Harkta's hopes and fears and desires, and no more likely to do her bidding than the wizard himself. Only she and Harkta and Weiland knew that.

But to Owen, both Harktas were doing exactly what she had ordered: They were looking like they didn't know what she was talking about.

"Back," Owen quietly ordered his men.

The men fell back, fingering their weapons.

"Now see here," Harkta said. "This creature does not take her orders."

The second Harkta said: "That's true."

"Which—?" one of the guards asked.

"Me." Harkta pointed to himself. "I'm the original. That one's perfectly harmless, but kill it if that'll make you feel better."

"No!" the other said, Harkta's instinct for self-preservation strong in it. No matter that it would fade away before dawn, it didn't want to die now. "*I'm* the original."

"See here." Harkta laughed nervously. "Owen. Friend. It's me. Just this afternoon, we stood in Lord Theron's chamber and toasted to our success." He forced a confident grin.

"'Excelsior,' we said," the fetch finished.

Owen's eyes flicked from one to the other.

"Magic?" Harkta offered. "Shall I prove it's me by doing magic?"

"Kill them both," Owen ordered.

Harkta, his hands raised in the opening gesture of a spell, and the fetch, turning to flee the room, both cried, "It's me!"

Lylene heard the *twang* of two crossbows releasing, then two muffled thuds. Both Harktas dropped to the floor.

Pain slammed into her heart. She staggered, moaning, and for one instant Harkta's fetch's fear was her fear; she shared his surprise, his denial, his pain. The room whirled and blackened.

The guard behind jerked on her collar, forcing her upright, leaving her panting and drained. Hearing returned, then sight. She felt her hands being tied behind her back, never having heard Owen give the order, never having seen Owen approach the lifeless bodies, though he was there now, with an expression of mild distaste on his face.

"Well," he said, "that'll save Theron a fat fee, so he won't be complaining." He stopped in front of Weiland. "Now for you. Where is he?"

"Who?"

"Your companion."

"Dead." Weiland looked away. "He died in the dungeon."

"Don't"—Owen held a finger in Weiland's face—"think our friendship is going to save you. I just came from the dungeon. He's not there—only four of our guards and one old man who has yet to be accounted for."

That hurt, more than Lylene would have thought.

"The old man is Shile. He—"

Owen nodded, and the guard behind kicked the back of Weiland's knee.

Weiland dropped.

With his left hand Owen yanked Weiland's short-cropped hair at the neck, forcing his head down. His right hand raised the sword. "No time for this nonsense. Last chance."

Lylene saw Weiland brace himself for the blow.

Owen saw it too and took that for his answer.

"It's true!" she cried as Owen heaved the sword up another handspan. "I did it magically. Stop!"

Owen slammed the sword down. The blade whistled through the air hitting the floor with enough force to chip the wooden planking.

Barely its own width in front of Weiland's face.

Owen jerked on Weiland's hair again, this time forcing his head back, forcing him to look up. "Suicidal fool!" he screamed.

Weiland, for once, was scared, was breathing hard.

"I thought you had more sense than that. I thought you were smart enough not to get yourself killed over some stupid whore of a girl." Owen gave one last angry yank on his hair.

Weiland looked as though his nerves were strung as far as they could go. He wouldn't be able to go through that again. All Owen had to do was ask, she thought, and Weiland would tell him everything, switch sides, anything.

Owen didn't ask. Instead, he said to the guards, "I'd better get Lord Theron's approval before something that irrevocable. You"—he indicated one—"go down to Hall and explain the situation. The rest of you, bring the bodies, so he can judge the likeness for himself."

One of the guards hesitated. "Leaving you—" he started.

"With two bound prisoners," Owen finished. "I think I can handle that."

Owen waited till they were alone in the room. Then, shaking his head, he used his sword to cut Weiland's bonds. "I swear this is it," he said. "Never again. We ever meet on opposite sides again, and I swear I'll kill you."

Weiland's reactions were uncharacteristically sluggish.

Owen dragged him to his feet and flung him toward the door. He cut Lylene's ropes and pushed her after him. "What the hell you want—an armed escort? Go. Get out of here. Try to keep out of Theron's way because if he captures you and sends you to me, I *will* kill you."

Weiland stiffened his arms out, preventing Owen from pushing him through the doorway. "What about you?"

"God's teeth! Do I have the entire garrison out searching the castle for me? I'll be fine if you just get the hell out of here. I'll say you got loose and overpowered me." He shoved them both toward the door. "Forget the slut," he advised Weiland.

It hurt, even though she knew he had every reason to believe it.

"And kindly don't steal any of the castle silver on your way out."

"Our swords," Weiland said.

As Owen turned toward the bed where the guards had thrown their weapons, Weiland slammed his elbow into the side of Owen's head. Owen staggered and Weiland hit him again. Owen dropped to the floor.

Lylene looked at Weiland in horror as he went to fetch the swords himself. Seeing her expression, he said, "He'll survive. They'd have never believed we overpowered him if he didn't have a mark on him."

It was obvious, and she was chagrined with herself for not realizing that, for thinking . . . But Weiland seemed to encourage that kind of thinking.

He fastened his sword belt before things apparently all caught up to him at once. He leaned against the wall with his hands on his knees, having trouble catching his breath. He looked up at her and shook his head.

She put her back to the opposite wall, suddenly weak herself. "You were prepared to die."

He regarded her blankly.

"Harkta's prophecy." She spoke between great shuddering breaths. "He never said you *would* die. Just that you had to be prepared to die."

Weiland looked as though he were seriously considering strangling all wizards, starting with her.

"Let's get out of here," she said. "Before Owen's messengers come back."

20

They traveled at a run, through corridors, up stairs and down, outside the main building, then back in.

Weiland finally paused in front of a door, checking to make sure no one was watching, then pulled her in. The smoothness of the move was balanced by the fact that he had to go back out to get a torch so they could see.

She removed her helmet, which was heavy and overly warm. They were in a room that was obviously used for weapons storage.

Weiland pulled a crossbow from its hanging place on the wall. "Know how to use one of these?"

She shook her head.

"I'll show you."

"I'm not very strong."

He put the weapon in her hands. "You don't have to be strong to use a crossbow. You don't have to be clever or skilled. You're supposed to be gentry, but I never let that stop me." He positioned her hands, then moved behind her, supporting her arms.

Lylene stiffened against his touch. Relax, she told herself. It was only Weiland, who had no designs on her body but was innocently teaching her how to kill more efficiently. She let him reposition his hands beneath her elbows, taking some of the weight of the crossbow.

"Sight." He pointed. "Trigger. Crank. The arrow—the bolt—fits in here, like this." He reached around to show her.

He won't hurt me, she told herself; but she already knew that. Overall, the sensation was a pleasant one, and that was what scared her. How could Weiland have this effect on her? She wished, as she had used to wish when she was a little girl—before she had seen it was useless—that she could be pretty.

"Higher. If it slips, you'll release into your foot. See this? All right, back. That's the way." He pointed out the window, to a target leaning against the wall that surrounded the keep. "See that bullseye?"

"I can't—"

Weiland turned her around, his cheek almost touching hers, his arms around her, supporting her. "Steady. It'll kick back a bit. *Don't* close your eyes. Steady. Release."

The release did throw her back against him, but the bolt hit the target, which was a surprise.

"Good. Try it again. Keep your eyes on the target, even after you release." He stepped back for her to do it on her own.

She told herself she missed his touch because she wouldn't be able to do it without him.

She hit the target, though not in the center this time.

He handed her another bolt.

This time she got it loaded more smoothly and it hit between the first and second shots.

Weiland reached around her again. "Here," he said. "Pull it up closer—"

She turned her face to look at him just as he turned to look at her. "Pull it up closer," he repeated, softly, "like this." That shown, he stepped away, his eyes downcast.

This arrow landed almost in the center.

"You're a born archer," he said. But he suddenly sounded as awkward, as self-conscious, as she felt. And he avoided her eyes, which he had never done before.

Weiland selected a wooden bow for himself, and two quivers—one of arrows, the other crossbow bolts. "You don't want to over-practice and tire your arms out." He glanced at the door. "We better get going."

She took two deep breaths.

He tossed the torch in the corner by the wooden practice-shields. The flame sputtered, caught, began to grow.

"You're becoming alarmingly fond of setting fires lately." It wasn't what she wanted to say.

He stood by the door waiting, and she didn't say anything else.

Again they went running through the castle passageways.

A man, an unarmored knight or servant, opened a door. A moment later and they would have run into it. "Hey!" the man called after them. "Where—"

Weiland turned, raising his bow, and fired.

The man toppled behind the door, and Lylene had no idea whether he was injured and hiding or dead.

Weiland slowed long enough to ready another arrow, not long at all, then picked up the pace again.

They stopped short of the last door. Weiland whispered even though the noise from the room was loud enough that he probably could have shouted and gone unnoticed. "You fire to get their attention. I'll keep them covered."

They stepped through the open doorway.

There were several entrances to the Great Hall. Weiland had chosen one that opened above. Stairs followed the curve of the outside wall, leading down into the huge room. A strategic position, she recognized, easy to defend. The air was thick with smoke. Her eyes took a moment to adjust. Her ears were assailed by the din: many conversations going on at once while servants clearing off the tables clattered dishes. Someone strummed a stringed instrument. Two large dogs were fighting over something found under one of the tables, and in their struggles they pulled down the cloth and the platters still on it.

Owen's men had to have arrived before them. Apparently the death of the wizard hadn't been considered worth interrupting supper for.

She could see why Weiland had told her to get their attention. Nobody even noticed them.

She surveyed the crowd. There. There was Beryl. She appeared unharmed. She sat at the main table in a low-cut green gown, her pale blonde hair in a multitude of intricate braids that framed her flushed and pretty face.

And that, sitting next to her, his arm draped over her shoulder so that his hand came close to resting on her breast, that must be Theron. Skinny blond moustache, cold blue eyes.

Lylene concentrated on keeping her arms steady, and sighted.

Weiland leaned down to put his mouth by her ear. "We don't want Theron dead."

"We don't?"

"Kill him like this, and be prepared to be hunted for the rest of your short miserable life. Church and King and people who for years have wanted Theron dead will be after you."

She spared him a sidelong glance.

"*Not this way,*" he insisted. "Not like some sneak assassin. Proclaim yourself."

"*Chivalry,* Weiland?"

"For our own protection."

"And then?"

"And then anything. But proclaim yourself first."

Weiland was always, she reminded herself, the one with both feet on the ground.

She found Theron's coat of arms hanging on the wall behind the table and sighted on that. Steady. Eyes on. She released.

The bolt cut through the thick smoky air with a hiss and thudded into the snout of the boar's head mounted to the right of the coat of arms.

No matter. It did get their attention.

Immediate silence. Broken only by the dogs, still snarling and circling each other, their nails clicking on the flagstones until someone reached down and cuffed one of them.

All those eyes, looking up, looking at her. And at Weiland with his bowstring drawn back, poised and ready while she reloaded.

Theron got to his feet and motioned his men not to try anything—at least for the moment.

Weiland stepped back, so that Lylene was in the forefront. She wanted Theron to know what was happening. And why. "Do you know who I am, *Lord* Theron?"

"The Lady Lylene Delroy of Dorstede." She thought she detected the slightest hint of a quaver in his voice. "My wife's sister."

"Just so you know." Lylene brought the crossbow up the way Weiland had shown her.

"Lylene! No!"

Lylene paused at the familiar voice. "Beryl?" She lowered the bow slightly. She was aware of Weiland still beside her, still with his bow drawn.

Her sister stepped forward from behind the table. Stepped forward to Theron's side. "Lylene, don't. You don't understand."

Lylene looked at the pretty, upturned face, at the golden hair. "Get away from him!" she warned, for he could easily grab Beryl and use her as a shield.

"Lylene, sister, listen. Theron's been kind to me—"

"He's responsible for Shile dying!" Lylene cried. This wasn't going at all the way it should have. "He killed Aunt Mathilde."

Beryl ignored the first part, as she always ignored what she didn't understand. "I heard about Mathilde, Lylene. But it was an accident."

"Accident?" Lylene cried. "How can you call what happened at Delroy an accident? Was the arrow they shot through your husband's heart an accident?"

Beryl looked close to putting on the pout she

had worn whenever Lylene refused to play by her constantly changing rules. "Lylene, Randal is not the point. The point is Theron is a kind and gentle man who has treated me very well . . ."

She kept on talking, but Lylene stopped hearing. Theron had treated her well, Theron had treated her well: The words went round and round Lylene's head. She had seen the fine furnishings in her sister's room, the exquisite hangings in the Hall—all mirroring Beryl's tastes. Suddenly the gown of green silk embroidered with gold seemed to Lylene a more grown-up version of the kind of dresses Beryl had always favored.

Weiland moved closer, so that his arm was against hers, solid reassurance, steadying her.

Beryl stood below, her hand resting lightly on the front of her gown, her face chubby and content, her breasts full and rosy where the gown was cut low, and the gown . . . the gown . . .

Lylene noticed for the first time what should have been readily apparent: that Beryl was heavy with child; her time must be near. "You're expecting a baby," she blurted out.

Beryl stopped what she was saying, closed her eyes and sighed. "Yes, dear sister, I'm expecting a baby."

"And you're protecting this man—*this man*—who killed the father of your child?"

"Lylene!" Beryl stamped her foot, as Beryl

was always wont to do. "Lylene, Theron *is* the father."

Lylene's hand shook on the bow. That seemed all the more reason . . . But she was obviously missing something. If Randal . . . If Theron . . . Beryl had only been gone eight months . . . She felt icy fingers stroke her soul. "When is the baby due?"

"Lylene—"

"*When is the baby due?*"

Beryl turned pale. She stepped away from Theron, putting space between herself and trouble. "Lylene," she said, tipping her head prettily to one side, as she had done since childhood.

"You planned it," Lylene said. "The two of you planned it. You murdered Randal so you could get his lands and titles, and you didn't care how many other people got killed along the way."

"That's not true," Theron said. "Some of my men got out of control, and I had them properly disciplined." He moved closer to Beryl, who sidestepped away from him.

"*I* told him it wasn't a good plan," Beryl said. "You can't believe *I*'d have anything to do with killing people."

"You murderer!" Lylene whispered, cutting off the protest Theron was about to start. She swung the bow up. "I gave up everything for you! People have died for you!" She realigned the arrow, aiming for Beryl's ivory throat. She found the trigger. She watched Beryl's hand scrabble for Theron's. *"People have died for you!"* She drew back the trigger and released.

Just as Weiland jostled her arm.

The arrow angled up and sideways, struck one of the banners, then dropped to the floor.

"Sorry," Weiland murmured, his bow still aimed and at the ready. "Shall I go down and hold her for you, do you think, to make sure you hit her this time?"

Lylene's shaking got out of control. "Damn you," she said to him. The crossbow fell from her numb fingers. She turned and ran.

"Back off!" she heard Weiland snarl at someone. And then he was in the corridor running beside her. "Lady, this way."

"Let go of me." She beat at his hands.

"Lady," he said between clenched teeth and shook her. "Do you want to die, or do you want to live?" It was just like Weiland to cut through to the basics.

"I want to live," she conceded.

21

He dragged her to a narrow archer's loop, and for a moment she feared he was going to try to get her to squeeze through and either jump or climb down. Instead, he only leaned out and shouted: "Fire! Fire in weapons storage! Sound the alarm!"

Without waiting for a reaction, he took off again.

Outside, a bell started ringing. "Why *up*?" she shouted as they started up a flight of stairs.

"Because they'll be guarding all the downstairs exits." He let go her arm and threw open a window shutter. "Go." He lifted her through the window and onto the rampart walk, a jump no higher than from a horse. Immediately she crouched below the level of the parapet, and in an instant he was beside her.

They peeked over the edge. The soldiers' quarters were almost directly beneath. Smoke poured into the night sky from the fire Weiland had set, and guards and servants had already begun to rush back and forth with water buckets.

Weiland tapped her shoulder, motioned for her to follow.

They ran at a half crouch because the wall was crenellated for defense: high, wide merlons to hide behind, spaced by narrow embrasures from which to shoot. All anybody below needed to do was look up at the wrong moment . . .

They rounded to the northern face of the keep, and here Weiland slowed.

"What's—"

He cut her off with a glare. He was studying the parapet. Counting, she realized, just as he stopped at one of the merlons. He reached up to the top and brought down a coil of rope, which he proceeded to tie around the merlon.

She looked through the opening. It was a long, long way down.

Weiland wrapped the other end of the rope around his waist, put his arm through the bowstring and slung the bow around his back. "I'll go first. You come down at the same time, so I can help support your weight."

She nodded, hoping he didn't notice she was shivering. "Lucky the excitement is away from where you hid the rope," she whispered. Then, as he tugged to make sure the rope was secure: "Or did you plan to set that fire all along?"

"No." Weiland went over the side, and the

rope went taut. He braced his feet against the wall. "Take the rope. Spread your hands. Come on, swing over: I'll support you. *Don't close your eyes.*"

She tore her attention away from the ground and concentrated on the length of rope above Weiland's hands.

"Lady."

It all came down to whether she trusted him. She squeezed through the embrasure, felt her heart go in one direction, her stomach in another, and then Weiland had an arm around her waist and his shoulder under her rump.

"Get your feet against the wall. Hand under hand—if you slide, the rope will burn."

"I'm all right," she assured him. "How did you happen to choose here to hide your rope?"

"I didn't. I hid one on each face."

She started to look at him but caught a glimpse of treetops and far-off ground. "I thought you said Shile always did all the planning." They seemed to be plummeting down the sheer side. "You're moving too fast."

He didn't counter that she was moving too slow.

Just when she thought it couldn't get worse—with the rope biting into her hands, and her arms and shoulders straining—he said, "The rope isn't long enough. We'll have to jump."

"What?" She finally looked earthward and saw that they were only thirty or forty hands up.

"Hold on. Don't slide."

She had thought she was doing a good job of supporting her own weight, but as soon as he was gone, she felt the almost unbearable tug on her arms.

"All right, let go," he called. "I'll catch you."

There was the possibility that she could break both legs if he missed. She took a deep breath and let go.

He caught her.

She held onto him even after she caught her balance and her breath. "Owen meant her," she said. "I thought he was talking about me. When he said you shouldn't be risking your life for a whore."

"Lady . . ." He shook his head helplessly.

She finally let go of him. "What now?"

He sighed. "Try to scale the outer wall, I guess. Theron will have his men coming out the front, and the fire brigade's taken over the back."

"Scale the wall?" she asked. "If they don't pick us off while we're still trying to make it up there, then we'll walk home?"

He folded his arms, waiting.

"The people putting out the fire don't look very well organized. Shile . . . Shile would have gone up to them waving his arms, talking loud and fast, given them some orders, and circled around past to the stables."

"I'm . . . not Shile," he said.

"And I can't talk or they'll know I'm not a guard."

In the end they had no choice but to do it her way.

They came round into the inner bailey at a run, Weiland swearing loudly. "Who's in charge here?" he bellowed. "What is this? Can't you move any faster? Keep that line straight. Can't they get the water out here any faster?" The louder he shouted, the more the workers tried to stay out of his way. "You"—he pointed at Lylene—"come with me, and we'll see what can be done."

They dodged through the line of workers and headed off in the direction of the well, which was also the direction of the stables.

"Fire!" Weiland shouted, any stablemaster's nightmare. "Burning embers on the roof."

Only one man came out—apparently Theron hadn't gotten here to post guards yet. Lylene pointed to the roof, and the man stepped back to see. Weiland dropped the bow off his back and nocked an arrow.

"Where?" the guard was demanding. "I see no sm—"

The arrow hit him in the back, and he toppled without a sound.

"Why couldn't you just have knocked him out?" Lylene demanded as Weiland dragged him into the stable, out of view.

He counted out on his fingers: "One, too risky. Two, we'll be in here too long. Three, don't question my methods. *Don't,*" he added as she opened her mouth—"say anything."

She didn't. Instead, while Weiland saddled the horses, she walked up and down the aisles making duplicates of Theron's horses.

Weiland finally looked up. "*What are you doing?*" he demanded.

"Hopefully, confusing Theron's men. I just put a little bit of power into those duplicates. Anybody that chooses a made horse to come after us will find himself on foot in a very short while."

He swore, softly, still distrustful of her sorcery.

She held up the knife he had given her. "I've also been slashing saddle girths."

This time he did flash a smile. "Good work. Get up."

She realized he'd saddled Shile's horse. She shook her head. "I can't ride him. Where's Harkta's?"

"This is the better horse."

"That makes no difference if I can't ride it."

"He's well trained, and he'll follow mine. All you have to do is hold on."

"Shall we flip a coin for it?"

"Will you get on the goddamn horse?"

She got on the horse.

They rode as fast as they thought they could without raising suspicion.

"Is there a postern gate?" she called to him.

"No."

That left the way they had come in, through the barbican. There had been two guards then, plus, presumably, one in the upper room which housed the mechanism for the drop-gate.

As they approached, Weiland shouted up to the guards: "Did they get out? Has anyone lowered the portcullis?"

Five guards stepped out of the shadows, three armed with crossbows, two with swords.

"Have you lowered the portcullis?" Weiland demanded again. "What's the matter with you? Give the order."

The guards hesitated, and by then Weiland and Lylene were too close. "The bowmen," Weiland told her, and she aimed her horse at one of those guards, praying that the man had the sense to get out of her way.

Weiland drew his sword, and he slashed at one of the bowmen, then rode down a second.

The last scrambled to get out of Lylene's path. He released the bolt too quickly, and it flew harmlessly against the barbican wall. Shile's horse reared, recognizing attack and flailing his hooves at it. Lylene held on with hands and knees and will. She thought the guardsman was hit, but didn't know for certain. Didn't want to know for certain.

Weiland had wheeled his horse around and was going after the two swordsmen.

There was still, Lylene knew, a guard in the upstairs room. She caught a glimpse of movement through the *meurtrière,* the hole in the ceiling: the guard positioning himself with a crossbow. She tugged on her horse's reins, causing it to sidestep toward the wall. She grabbed a torch from its bracket and flung it up into the hole. She heard the guard curse and knock the torch away. "Weiland!" she called and pointed up.

He had killed the remaining two guards and now leapt from his horse's back, swinging up on top of the barbican and scrambling into the windlass-control room through the window.

Lylene grabbed another torch, duplicating it even as she threw it up into the *meurtrière*. She made another, threw that one also, hoping that she was distracting the guard more than hampering Weiland.

Through the barbican, from the direction of the keep, she could hear men yelling and horses galloping. No sight of them yet. She made another torch.

"Lady. Enough. Keep one." Weiland reached

down from the opening to take the other from her. "Ride out to the other side of the drawbridge."

"But—"

"Start duplicating that torch, and drop them onto the drawbridge."

"Guards are coming. What are you doing?"

"I'm trying to set this torch so that it'll burn the windlass ropes after we're out but before anybody else can pass through."

"Hurry." If Weiland mistimed, the portcullis would drop and trap him in the castle. She urged her mount through the barbican, gazing up, as she passed, to see the spiked ends of the gate. If Weiland mistimed badly enough, the portcullis would drop while he was passing under it.

She started doubling torches, letting them fall on the wooden drawbridge.

She heard the thud as Weiland dropped down from the upper room. Behind him, she could now see the approaching mounted guard, about fifteen men, with a second, larger, party behind.

Weiland swung onto his horse, keeping low. Two crossbow bolts flew past where his head would have been if he'd been sitting upright. "Go!" he shouted at her. But she stayed to see him make it past the deadly portcullis. His horse clattered over the drawbridge, disregarding the fires. "I said *go*—dammit, don't you ever listen?"

An arrow whistled between them.

She put heels to the horse's sides, but Weiland had been right: The horses knew they belonged together. Shile's horse had started even before she moved, as soon as Weiland passed, and quickly lengthened its stride until the ground flew precariously beneath them.

More arrows flew at them, the mounted archers' aim shaken by the speed they were traveling.

There was a crash and the unmistakable screaming of a horse in pain: Weiland's torch had eaten through the rope.

She saw Weiland check over his shoulder. She didn't dare—not at the speed they were traveling. Somebody must have made it through the gate and over the drawbridge, for he didn't slow down. They were passing through the outlying farms, and no cover in sight.

Another flurry of arrows, fewer this time, and almost spent. Weiland glanced back once, then a second time, then pulled his horse to a stop. Shile's horse stopped, either because she pulled up on the reins or because Weiland's had.

She turned.

Behind them, six knights were on foot—and, from the look of them, very suddenly on foot.

Saddles and equipment were strewn on the ground with them—but no sign of any horses. A seventh knight was still mounted, but finding himself the lone pursuer, had decided to turn back.

Lylene leaned forward, exhausted but unable to keep the satisfied grin off her face as she turned to Weiland.

He saw her watching him, and wheeled his horse about. "That downed gate and burned drawbridge aren't going to hold them back forever," he said.

"You're welcome," she answered.

22

"The trouble with relatives," Weiland said when they felt safe enough to let the horses—and themselves—rest, "is that nobody checks beforehand to see whether you want them."

"I don't have any relatives," Lylene said.

"Neither do I," Weiland said. "But Shile . . ." He didn't finish that thought. When he finally spoke again, it was only to ask, "What are your plans?"

She was unable to make anything of the tone. Or the expression either. She had never thought beyond Beryl before. "My aunt is . . . was . . . a friend of the abbess at the convent of Saint Marcelle sur la Mer." She probably would have ended up there anyway, once Beryl was settled. Now that she realized she owed the Bishop of Glastonbury an apology, now that she realized that the Church hadn't been plotting against her but had simply recognized the situation for what it was. . . . It wouldn't be a bad life—

quiet, provided for. Not what she'd been used to the past several months. She'd learned a lot, and some of that she'd have to work very hard to forget.

Weiland said nothing, and she turned to face him. He was sitting on a downed tree, making aimless patterns in the dirt with a stick. There was a faint breeze, which played with his hair, whose shortness was a constant reminder of what they'd been through.

She rubbed her sweaty palm on her breeches. (Shile's breeches, Shile's horse, Shile's Phoenician coin.) "I don't have anyplace else to go." She could have kicked herself for admitting that. It sounded as though she wanted him to take her under his care, which was, of course, totally inappropriate, and anyway, he was bound to say no.

He didn't answer. What could he have said?

"How about you?" she asked.

"I don't know. Set off north, I guess."

"What's north?"

He shrugged. "I've never been there."

"Ahh," she said, trying to sound as though that was promising, trying to sound as though he'd said he was really a baron's son with inherited lands waiting for him.

They weren't good for each other, she told herself. They were too different, and neither would ever understand the other.

"Do you *want* to be a religious?" Weiland asked.

It was the safe thing to do, and would only cost her freedom. "No," she admitted. She had learned she didn't need anyone to take care of her. She had her magic, and surely people made their way in the world with less.

"We could . . . If you wanted . . . Maybe it might . . ." Weiland closed his eyes, obviously unused to and frustrated by this inarticulation. "I thought, maybe . . ."

Make your wager, she thought. *Hope for the best. And throw the dice.*

"Yes," she agreed.

He released a breath.

"Work together?" she supplied. "See how it goes? Nothing definite, nothing permanent, just until something better comes along for either of us?"

He nodded, slowly.

"Yes," she repeated.

He had a nice smile, actually, when he wasn't scowling.

She didn't let that distract her. "On condition."

"What," he said, "condition?"

"Well, for one thing, I will not use my magic power to make temporary money to pay our way."

He considered, then gave a terse nod.

"For another thing," she went on before he could say a word, "I would appreciate your not stabbing or shooting people in the back any more than absolutely necessary."

He folded his arms across his chest.

"And then there's your language."

"My what?"

"It's probably no worse than half the other men in the country, but you've got to consider my background: I find it offensive to hear the name of our Lord and Savior used casually or in anger."

She almost lost him there. He took a deep breath. Looked at her levelly. Then finally said, "I will try. Is there anything else you don't like?"

"Well, I'm not especially fond of that narrow-eyed look you're giving me right now, but I suppose I can live with it."

"Jes—" Weiland started, but bit it off. "I have a condition too."

It was Lylene's turn to hold her breath.

"That you refrain from questioning every move I make."

Lylene released her breath. "I will try," she agreed.

And she did.

Though it was easier some days than others.

Here is an excerpt from the sequel to
The Conjurer Princess

The Changeling Prince

by Vivian Vande Velde

forthcoming from HarperPrism

Chapter One

Weiland woke up naked, in the snow, in a part of the forest he didn't recognize, with blood in his mouth. His last clear memory was settling down to sleep by the fire in Daria's hall.

But there were other memories that weren't clear—vague and dark and familiar memories—which argued with his impression that he had done nothing wrong, that he had given Daria no reason to punish him.

Though that was never a guarantee with Daria in any case.

Still, he tried to convince himself that this could conceivably be a prank by Lon or one of the others, that they might have thought it humorous to pick him up while he slept, to carry him outdoors. . . .

It didn't make sense. As near as he'd ever been able to work out, Weiland was sixteen years old, with most of those years spent in Daria's household. Sixteen years had made a light sleeper of him precisely because it was the sort of thing they *would* find humorous.

He could no longer ignore the pain in his right leg, which was more than the cold could account for. He raised himself on his arms, and looked. His ankle was held fast by the teeth of a metal wolf trap, which was certainly beyond what even Lon would dare. And besides, he could see the tracks, padded and four-footed in the snow, which ended at the impression his own body had made. He had apparently already struggled: the trap's teeth had worked their way down to the bone in ragged gouges that went from knee to ankle. Still, bad as the injury looked, it wasn't enough to account for the blood in his mouth, which had been his last desperate hope.

His stomach clenched in on itself. He managed to get to almost sitting before he began to vomit. The spasms brought up—as he had known they would—raw meat, barely chewed.

A wolf's meal.

There was a time when he'd have examined what his stomach brought up, frantic to find fur or hollow birds' bones, proof that he hadn't preyed on humans while possessed of a wolf's body. But Lon had caught him at it, and gloated that he'd witnessed Weiland's killing a small child, once when Weiland had stayed a wolf long enough to digest what he'd devoured. Of course, anything Lon said was suspect, and particularly this, since everyone knew what Weiland was most afraid of hearing. *Liar,* Weiland called him. *Fool,* Lon retaliated. It had ended, eventually, with Daria punishing both of them, though in some moods she enjoyed seeing her company fight. But this time she had turned Weiland once more into a wolf, and—since Lon enjoyed his true form, a bear—*his* sentence had been to forego his supper. *Liar,* Weiland had said. But since then, he no longer looked for proof that he hadn't killed a human, for fear he might find proof of exactly the opposite.

He continued heaving even after his stomach was empty, first bringing up throat-burning bile, then nothing, until he felt as though each convulsion would bring up his stomach itself.

Finally finished, he rested his face in the crook of his arm, covered with sweat despite the freezing air, which was surely more danger to him than anything he'd eaten, anything he'd done, while in the form of a wolf. There were tears in his eyes, but that was purely from exertion, not from the pain caused by inadvertently jerking his leg so that the trap's metal teeth scraped against bone, and certainly not from emotion.

The fact that Daria wasn't there to see meant

nothing: Daria didn't believe in crying. Daria had beaten all the crying out of Weiland by the time he was four. That was when she had first told him that the pelt on her bed was his mother. He didn't remember his mother, he didn't remember roaming the woods as a wolf cub or Daria capturing him or her working that first humanizing transformation on him. In fact, he had spent more of his growing years human than wolf, which might have been why he alone—of all Daria's creatures—preferred his human form. But he'd cried when he learned about his mother, and Daria had beaten him badly enough that she had to work her healing magic on him afterward, or he would have died.

Now he struggled to remember: what could he have done this time that Daria would wait until he was asleep, then work a transformation on him in her own hall? Surely that had to be inconvenient—dangerous, even—for when he was a wolf he forgot what it was to be human. The sudden thought that what he had just vomited may well have been one of his companions caused his stomach to spasm again.

When the cold was enough to cut through his misery, he sat up—carefully, so as not to drag his leg further through the trap—and he took a handful of snow to clear the tastes of blood and vomit from his mouth.

It was so cold, it was akin to burning.

But he'd already waited too long to start worrying about getting loose, if he'd ever had a chance. The blood loss, the vomiting, the shivering that had set in from the cold—all conspired to make him too weak to pry open the jaws of the trap. His fingers stuck to the metal. Skin tore loose, but feeling was already going. And even if he should get free of the trap, what then? Either Daria knew exactly where he was and would fetch him when she estimated he'd learned whatever lesson she thought he needed to learn. Or she didn't know—and that would leave little enough likelihood of his finding shelter within the distance he could travel, even assuming the bone wasn't broken.

Weiland lay back down and trusted to his luck, despite the knowledge that if he were truly lucky, he wouldn't be there. He clenched his fists to hold as much warmth as he could in his fingers, and pulled his knees up to his chest, as well as he could without dragging agianst the trap.

Surely, he told himself, the fact that he was in human form proved that Daria was nearby, working her magic on him, for Daria readily admitted that there was a geographic limit beyond which her magic wouldn't reach. Surely, Daria just wanted to make him suffer longer. Even if he lost fingers or toes to the cold, even if he were on the point of dying, her magic would heal him. It had before.

As the cold made him grow sleepy despite fear and pain, he wondered if Daria's magic was strong enough to raise the dead.

It was a bad thought to drift off with, for someone who hoped to be lucky enough to die.

Chapter Two

He wasn't dead.

Daria's voice came from far away—flitting up and down and around corners to reach him. "This is going to be quite painful."

Weiland didn't need Daria's warning. Her healings often hurt worse than the original injuries: burning, ripping, bone-scraping power that skittered and clawed over his entire body, leaving him panting and too weak to rise from his bed for days, even the time he'd only started out with a sprained wrist. But she'd been annoyed, on that occasion, when he'd been unable to serve at dinner, the platters too heavy for his unsteady grip. The fact that her magic made him unfit to serve for two additional days meant nothing to her.

She must be mightily annoyed this time, too, Weiland realized in the moments of clarity between dizziness and pain: She had obviously healed him enough that he could hear and understand, taking this in stages rather than wasting the pain on someone too far gone to feel it.

Her cool soft fingers gently brushed his sweat-dampened hair from his forehead. Not that there was that much hair: Swordmaster Kedj made them all keep their hair cropped short so that an enemy couldn't catch hold of it. Daria was just delaying, making sure he had his wits collected.

Weiland opened his eyes. He was in the hall, on his own sleeping pallet on the floor near the fireplace—the choice spot of Daria's company because—though he was the youngest—he'd been one of the longest in her household, and because since this last year he was strong enough to keep it.

Daria's face hovered a handspan from him; she was practically reclining next to him for the best possible view. She smiled. Daria was a beautiful woman, and her smile made Weiland think of love and kindness, though he'd had little enough experience of either. "Welcome back," she said. And let her magic loose on him.

It was always difficult to tell what Daria wanted. She might be watching so closely, so intently, because she was in the mood to see him writhing in agony. But Weiland instinctively bit back his outcry of pain, and Daria continued to caress his face. Apparently she was in the mood for him to be brave. Weiland had long ago learned to always give Daria whatever she wanted; it was just a matter of figuring out *what* she wanted.

By the time the worst of it was over, he was barely able to keep still, and he hadn't managed to be perfectly quiet. Still, Daria leaned forward and kissed him on the forehead before leaving, so she must have been pleased.

His breath still coming in shuddering gasps, Weiland drifted off, too lightheaded to find the blanket to pull up around him, too weak to close his fingers around it even if he had.

It was going to take a lot longer than two days to recover from this.

Days passed. Difficult to tell how many, and it made no difference anyway. One day was much the same as another in Daria's hall. Seasons differed, with the need for warmer or lighter clothing, with the availability of food, and the likelihood of travelers to intercept on their way over the hills. Days didn't differ, nor did years.

Gradually, Weiland became aware of being cold and realized the others had pulled him from his place by the fire while he couldn't retaliate.

Occasionally someone would surreptitiously kick him, or trod on his fingers as though by accident, but Daria must have been keeping some measure of watch, for his blanket didn't disappear, and he was kept clean and provided with water and—as he became stronger—broth.

Eventually, Weiland opened his eyes and once again found Daria watching him, this time from the full distance of her standing height. "Don't you think this is getting a bit excessive?" she asked. "If you can manage to rouse yourself, I want to speak to you."

Immediately Weiland sat up, though he was so lightheaded, he couldn't be sure he was upright.

Daria was gone by then. Weiland wasn't sure if he'd taken only the few moments it had seemed, or if he'd blacked out. Daria wouldn't take lightly being ignored. Regardless, Weiland was no sooner sitting up than he had to rest his head against his upraised knee.

Rohmar, passing by, stepped on the hand he was supporting himself with, which may or may not have been Rohmar's natural clumsiness.

But the others were watching. Lon among them. Waiting for a sign of weakness. Hungry for a sign of weakness.

Weiland hooked his leg around Rohmar's, causing him to topple, much to the delight of the others, even Lon—who had no doubt assumed the position of leadership within the hour of Weiland's having been brought back to the hall helpless. Lon wouldn't be concerned about who held which of the lower ranks.

Rohmar gave him a look of loathing. But Rohmar was a coward—Weiland thought he was more rabbit than wolf, though he had seen him made—and after a long moment, Rohmar averted his eyes, pretending to be preoccupied with rubbing his foot.

Weiland took a long, slow look around the hall. Without counting, still there was no one conspicuously absent. He had no friends here, no one whose death he would mourn; but there was a difference between that and not caring whether he had eaten one of them. Weiland didn't let this show in his face. His face showed only disdain. He ended with Lon, who grinned at him toothily probably never suspecting the relief, but knowing Weiland was in no condition to challenge him. Weiland felt bruised all over, as though he'd rolled down a mountain slope of rocks. But he grinned back. "After Daria," he said, trying to sound menacing. And confident that he could take on any of them. And at the same time, to remind everyone that Daria seemed to be currently interested in his well-being, and she would probably take it amiss if Lon ripped his head off. Weiland hoped Lon had reasoned things out similarly.

Lon didn't react at all, and Weiland pulled the blanket up around himself since there was no sign of the clothes he'd been wearing the last he could remember. When he stood, his legs almost gave out under him, which would have been a clear invitation for the others to jump him. Weakness was provocation in Daria's hall.

But he made it out of the hall without having to lean against walls or tables for support; and if their animal-born senses could hear the hammering of his heart and smell his feat and taste his pain, at least there was no way they could know that black shadows hovered at the edges of his vision.

Once he was out in the corridor, he kept moving because they might be watching. Or was that a human reaction? Sometimes he anticipated things that never occured, or worried about matters the others never seemed to consider, which may have been a result of being raised, for the most part, human. A waste of time, Daria told him. A failed experiment. Since him, she used full-grown animals, who were more dependable and cost less effort.

In any case, Weiland was not aware of any of the others following as he made his way to the storage room where Daria kept articles of clothing they took from travelers who didn't have enough money to pay the toll. Weiland sat on a chest and rested, breathing heavily.

Dressing exhausted him all over again, but he'd been too long already. Daria wasn't a patient woman. The leg which had been caught in the wolf trap throbbed despite the fact that it looked perfectly fit. Limping painfully, Weiland headed for Daria's rooms.

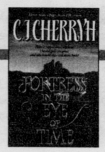